PENGUIN BOOKS

The Spy Who Loved Me

Ian Fleming was born in 1908 and educated at Eton and Sandhurst. He worked for a short time as a journalist with Reuters and at a City firm before joining the Foreign Office. He served in British Naval Intelligence during the Second World War. After the War he was Foreign Manager of the *Sunday Times*. The first of his James Bond thrillers, *Casino Royale*, was published in 1953. The titles that followed include *Live and Let Die* (1954), *Moonraker* (1955), *Diamonds are Forever* (1956), *From Russia with Love* (1957), *Goldfinger* (1959) and *You Only Live Twice* (1964). The books have sold more than sixty million copies to date and inspired the series of cult films. Fleming's own charming, confident personality and his life of world travel, gambling, fast cars and romance, along with his experience in wartime intelligence, drew inevitable parallels with his famous hero. He died of heart failure in 1964, at the age of 56, before James Bond had achieved the global recognition he now enjoys.

THE JAMES BOND BOOKS

Casino Royale

Live and Let Die

Moonraker

Diamonds are Forever

From Russia with Love

Dr No

Goldfinger

For Your Eyes Only

Thunderball

The Spy Who Loved Me

On Her Majesty's Secret Service

You Only Live Twice

The Man with the Golden Gun

Octopussy/The Living Daylights

The Spy Who Loved Me

IAN FLEMING

PENGUIN BOOKS

PENGUIN BOOKS

Published by the Penguin Group
Penguin Books Ltd, 80 Strand, London WC2R 0RL, England
Penguin Group (USA) Inc., 375 Hudson Street, New York, New York 10014, USA
Penguin Group (Canada), 90 Eglinton Avenue East, Suite 700, Toronto, Ontario, Canada M4P 2Y3
(a division of Pearson Penguin Canada Inc.)
Penguin Ireland, 25 St Stephen's Green, Dublin 2, Ireland (a division of Penguin Books Ltd)
Penguin Group (Australia), 250 Camberwell Road, Camberwell, Victoria 3124, Australia
(a division of Pearson Australia Group Pty Ltd)
Penguin Books India Pvt Ltd, 11 Community Centre, Panchsheel Park, New Delhi –110 017, India
Penguin Group (NZ), cnr Airborne and Rosedale Roads, Albany, Auckland 1310, New Zealand
(a division of Pearson New Zealand Ltd)
Penguin Books (South Africa) (Pty) Ltd, 24 Sturdee Avenue, Rosebank,
Johannesburg 2196, South Africa

Penguin Books Ltd, Registered Offices: 80 Strand, London WC2R 0RL, England

www.penguin.com

First published in Great Britain by Jonathan Cape Ltd 1962
First published in the United States by The Viking Press 1962
Published in Penguin Books (UK) 2002
Published in Penguin Books (USA) 2003
Published in Penguin Classics 2006
1

Printed in England by Clays Ltd, St Ives plc

ISBN-13: 978–0–141–18872–0
ISBN-10: 0–141–18872–3

CONTENTS

Part One / *Me*

1 / *SCAREDY CAT*

I was running away. I was running away from England, from my childhood, from the winter, from a sequence of untidy, unattractive love-affairs, from the few sticks of furniture and jumble of overworn clothes that my London life had collected around me; and I was running away from drabness, fustiness, snobbery, the claustrophobia of close horizons and from my inability, although I am quite an attractive rat, to make headway in the rat-race. In fact, I was running away from almost everything except the law.

And I had run a very long way indeed—almost, exaggerating a bit, halfway round the world. In fact, I had come all the way from London to The Dreamy Pines Motor Court which is ten miles west of Lake George, the famous American tourist resort in the Adirondacks—that vast expanse of mountains, lakes and pine forests which forms most of the northern territory of New York State. I had started on September 1st, and it was now Friday October 13th. When I had left, the grimy little row of domesticated maples in my square had been green, or as green as any tree can be in London in August. Now, in the billion-strong army of pine trees that marched away northwards towards the Canadian border, the real, wild maples flamed here and there like shrapnel-bursts. And I felt that I, or at any rate my skin, had changed just as much—from the grimy sallowness that had been the badge of my London life to the snap and colour and sparkle of living out of doors and going to bed early and all those other dear dull things that had been part of my life in Quebec before it was decided that I must go to England and learn to be a 'lady'. Very unfashionable, of course, this cherry-ripe, strength-through-joy complexion, and I had even stopped using lipstick and nail varnish, but to me it had been like sloughing off a borrowed skin and getting back into my own, and I was childishly happy and pleased with myself whenever I looked in the mirror (that's another thing—I'll never say 'looking-glass' again; I just don't have to any more) and found myself not wanting to paint a different face over my own. I'm not being smug about this. I was just running away from the person I'd been for the past five years. I wasn't particularly pleased with the person I was now, but I had hated and despised the other one, and I was glad to be rid of her face.

Station WOKO (they might have dreamed up a grander call-sign!) in Albany, the capital of New York State and about fifty miles due south of where I was, announced that it was six o'clock. The weather report that followed included a storm warning with gale-force winds. The storm was moving down from the north and would hit Albany around 8 pm. That meant that I would be having a noisy night. I didn't mind. Storms don't frighten me, and although the nearest living soul, as far as I knew, was ten miles away up the not very good secondary road to Lake George, the thought of the pines that would soon be thrashing outside, the thunder and lightning and rain, made me already feel snug and warm and protected in anticipation. And alone! But above all alone! 'Loneliness becomes a lover, solitude a darling sin.' Where had I read that? Who had written it? It was so exactly the way I felt, the way that, as a child, I had always felt until I had forced myself to 'get into the swim', 'be one of the crowd'—a good sort, on the ball, hep. And what a hash I had made of 'togetherness'! I shrugged the memory of failure away. Everyone doesn't have to live in a heap. Painters, writers, musicians are lonely people. So are statesmen and admirals and generals. But then, I added to be fair, so are criminals and lunatics. Let's just say, not to be too flattering, that true individuals are lonely. It's not a virtue, the reverse if anything. One ought to share and communicate if one is to be a useful member of the tribe. The fact that I was so much happier when I was alone was surely the sign of a faulty, a neurotic character. I had said this so often to myself in the past five years that now, that evening, I just shrugged my shoulders and, hugging my solitude to me, walked across the big lobby to the door and went out to have a last look at the evening.

I hate pine trees. They are dark and stand very still and you can't shelter under them or climb them. They are very dirty, with a most un-treelike black dirt, and if you get this dirt mixed with their resin they make you really filthy. I find their jagged shapes vaguely inimical, and the way they mass so closely together gives me the impression of an army of spears barring my passage. The only good thing about them is their smell, and, when I can get hold of it, I use pine-needle essence in my bath. Here, in the Adirondacks, the endless vista of pine trees was positively sickening. They clothe every square yard of earth in the valleys and climb up to the top of every mountain so that the impression is of a spiky carpet spread to the horizon—an endless vista of rather stupid-looking green pyramids waiting to be cut down for matches and coat-hangers and copies of the *New York Times*.

Five acres or so of these stupid trees had been cleared to build the motel, which is all that this place really was. 'Motel' isn't a good word any longer. It has become smart to use

'Motor Court' or 'Ranch Cabins' ever since motels became associated with prostitution, gangsters and murders, for all of which their anonymity and lack of supervision is a convenience. The site, tourist-wise, in the lingo of the trade, was a good one. There was this wandering secondary road through the forest, which was a pleasant alternative route between Lake George and Glens Falls to the south, and halfway along it was a small lake, cutely called Dreamy Waters, that is a traditional favourite with picnickers. It was on the southern shore of this lake that the motel had been built, its reception lobby facing the road with, behind this main building, the rooms fanning out in a semicircle. There were forty rooms with kitchen, shower and lavatory, and they all had some kind of a view of the lake behind them. The whole construction and design was the latest thing—glazed pitch-pine frontages and pretty timber roofs all over knobbles, air-conditioning, television in every cabin, children's playground, swimming pool, golf range out over the lake with floating balls (fifty balls, one dollar)—all the gimmicks. Food? Cafeteria in the lobby, and grocery and liquor deliveries twice a day from Lake George. All this for ten dollars single and sixteen double. No wonder that, with around two hundred thousand dollars' capital outlay and a season lasting only from July 1st to the beginning of October, or, so far as the NO VACANCY sign was concerned, from July 14th to Labour Day, the owners were finding the going hard. Or so those dreadful Phanceys had told me when they'd taken me on as receptionist for only thirty dollars a week plus keep. Thank heavens they were out of my hair! Song in my heart? There had been the whole heavenly choir at six o'clock that morning when their shiny station-wagon had disappeared down the road on their way to Glens Falls and then to Troy where the monsters came from. Mr Phancey had made a last grab at me and I hadn't been quick enough. His free hand had run like a fast lizard over my body before I had crunched my heel into his instep. He had let go then. When his contorted face had cleared, he said softly, 'All right, sex-box. Just see that you mind camp good until the boss comes to take over the keys tomorrow midday. Happy dreams tonight.' Then he had grinned a grin I hadn't understood, and had gone over to the station-wagon where his wife had been watching from the driver's seat. 'Come on, Jed,' she had said sharply. 'You can work off those urges on West Street tonight.' She put the car in gear and called over to me sweetly, ''Bye now, cutie-pie. Write us every day.' Then she had wiped the crooked smile off her face and I caught a last glimpse of her withered, hatchet profile as the car turned out on to the road. Phew! What a couple! Right out of a book—and what a book! Dear Diary! Well, people couldn't come much worse, and now they'd gone. From now on, on my travels, the human race *must* improve!

I had been standing there, looking down the way the Phanceys had gone, remembering them. Now I turned and looked to the north to see after the weather. It had been a beautiful day, Swiss clear and hot for the middle of October, but now high fretful clouds, black with jagged pink hair from the setting sun, were piling down the sky. Fast little winds were zigzagging among the forest tops and every now and then they hit the single yellow light above the deserted gas station down the road at the tail of the lake and set it swaying. When a longer gust reached me, cold and buffeting, it brought with it the whisper of a metallic squeak from the dancing light, and the first time this happened I shivered deliciously at the little ghostly noise. On the lake shore, beyond the last of the cabins, small waves were lapping fast against the stones and the gunmetal surface of the lake was fretted with sudden catspaws that sometimes showed a fleck of white. But, in between the angry gusts, the air was still, and the sentinel trees across the road and behind the motel seemed to be pressing silently closer to huddle round the camp-fire of the brightly-lit building at my back.

I suddenly wanted to go to the loo, and I smiled to myself. It was the piercing tickle that comes to children during hide-and-seek-in-the-dark and 'Sardines', when, in your cupboard under the stairs, you heard the soft creak of a floor-board, the approaching whisper of the searchers. Then you clutched yourself in thrilling anguish and squeezed your legs together and waited for the ecstasy of discovery, the crack of light from the opening door and then—the supreme moment—your urgent 'Ssh! Come in with me!', the softly closing door and the giggling warm body pressed tight against your own.

Standing there, a 'big girl' now, I remembered it all and recognized the sensual itch brought on by a fleeting apprehension—the shiver down the spine, the intuitive goose-flesh that come from the primitive fear-signals of animal ancestors. I was amused and I hugged the moment to me. Soon the thunderheads would burst and I would step back from the howl and chaos of the storm into my well-lighted, comfortable cave, make myself a drink, listen to the radio and feel safe and cosseted.

It was getting dark. Tonight there would be no evening chorus from the birds. They had long ago read the signs and disappeared into their own shelters in the forest, as had the animals—the squirrels and the chipmunks and the deer. In all this huge, wild area there was now only me out in the open. I took a last few deep breaths of the soft, moist air. The humidity had strengthened the scent of pine and moss, and now there was also a strong underlying armpit smell of earth. It was almost as if the forest was sweating with the same pleasurable excitement I was feeling. Somewhere, from quite close, a nervous owl asked loudly 'Who?' and then was silent. I took a few steps away from the lighted doorway and stood in the middle of the dusty road, looking north. A strong gust of wind hit me and blew back my hair. Lightning threw a quick blue-white hand across the horizon. Seconds later, thunder growled softly like a wakening guard dog, and then the big wind came and the tops of the trees began to dance and thrash and the yellow light over the gas station jigged and blinked down the road as if to warn me. It *was* warning me. Suddenly the dancing light was blurred with rain, its luminosity fogged by an advancing grey sheet of water. The first heavy drops hit me, and I turned and ran.

I banged the door behind me, locked it and put up the chain. I was only just in time. Then the avalanche crashed down and settled into a steady roar of water whose patterns of sound varied from a heavy drumming on the slanting timbers of the roof to a higher, more precise slashing at the windows. In a moment these sounds were joined by the busy violence of the overflow drainpipes. And the noisy background pattern of the storm was set.

I was still standing there, cosily listening, when the thunder, that had been creeping quietly up behind my back, sprang its ambush. Suddenly lightning blazed in the room, and at the same instant there came a block-busting crash that shook the building and made the air twang like piano wire. It was just one, single, colossal explosion that might have been a huge bomb falling only yards away. There was a sharp tinkle as a piece of glass fell out of one of the windows on to the floor, and then the noise of water pattering in on to the linoleum.

I didn't move. I couldn't. I stood and cringed, my hands over my ears. I hadn't meant it to be like this! The silence, that had been deafening, resolved itself back into the roar of the rain, the roar that had been so comforting but that now said,

'You hadn't thought it could be so bad. You had never seen a storm in these mountains. Pretty flimsy this little shelter of yours, really. How'd you like to have the lights put out as a start? Then the crash of a thunderbolt through that match-wood ceiling of yours? Then, just to finish you off, lightning to set fire to the place—perhaps electrocute you? Or shall we just frighten you so much that you dash out in the rain and try and make those ten miles to Lake George. Like to be alone do you? Well, just try this for size!' Again the room turned blue-white, again, just overhead, there came the ear-splitting crack of the explosion, but this time the crack widened and racketed to and fro in a furious cannonade that set the cups and glasses rattling behind the bar and made the woodwork creak with the pressure of the sound-waves.

My legs felt weak and I faltered to the nearest chair and sat down, my head in my hands. How could I have been so foolish, so, so impudent? If only someone would come, someone to stay with me, someone to tell me that this was only a storm! But it wasn't! It was catastrophe, the end of the world! And all aimed at *me*! Now! It would be coming again! Any minute now! I must do something, get help! But the Phanceys had paid off the telephone company and the service had been disconnected. There was only one hope! I got up and ran to the door, reaching up for the big switch that controlled the 'Vacancy/No Vacancy' sign in red neon above the threshold. If I put it to 'Vacancy', there might be someone driving down the road. Someone who would be glad of shelter. But, as I pulled the switch, the lightning, that had been watching me, crackled viciously in the room, and, as the thunder crashed, I was seized by a giant hand and hurled to the floor.

2 / *DEAR DEAD DAYS*

When I came to, I at once knew where I was and what had happened and I cringed closer to the floor, waiting to be hit again. I stayed like that for about ten minutes, listening to the roar of the rain, wondering if the electric shock had done me permanent damage, burned me, inside perhaps, making me unable to have babies, or turned my hair white. Perhaps all my hair had been burned off! I moved a hand to it. It felt all right, though there was a bump at the back of my head. Gingerly I moved. Nothing was broken. There was no harm. And then the big General Electric icebox in the corner burst into life and began its cheerful, domestic throbbing and I realized that the world was still going on and that the thunder had gone away and I got rather weakly to my feet and looked about me, expecting I don't know what scene of chaos and destruction. But there it all was, just as I had 'left' it—the important-looking reception desk, the wire rack of paperbacks and magazines, the long counter of the cafeteria, the dozen neat tables with rainbow-hued plastic tops and uncomfortable little metal chairs, the big ice-water container and the gleaming coffee percolator—everything in its place, just as ordinary as could be. There was only the hole in the window and a spreading pool of water on the floor as evidence of the holocaust through which this room and I had just passed. Holocaust? What was I talking about? The only holocaust had been in my head! There was a storm. There had been thunder and lightning. I had been terrified, like a child, by the big bangs. Like an idiot I had taken hold of the electric switch—not even waiting for the pause between lightning flashes, but choosing just the moment when another flash was due. It had knocked me out. I had been punished with a bump on the head. Served me right, stupid, ignorant scaredy cat! But wait a minute! Perhaps my hair *had* turned white! I walked, rather fast, across the room, picked up my bag from the desk and went behind the bar of the cafeteria and bent down and looked into the long piece of mirror below the shelves. I looked first inquiringly into my eyes. They gazed back at me, blue, clear, but wide with surmise. The lashes were there and the eyebrows, brown, an expanse of inquiring forehead and then, yes, the sharp, brown peak and the tumble of perfectly ordinary very dark brown hair curving away to right and left in two big waves. So! I took out my comb and ran it brusquely, angrily through my hair, put the comb back in my bag and snapped the clasp.

My watch said it was nearly seven o'clock. I switched on the radio, and while I listened to WOKO frightening its audience about the storm—power lines down, the Hudson River rising dangerously at Glens Falls, a fallen elm blocking Route 9 at Saratoga Springs, flood warning at Mechanicville—I strapped a bit of cardboard over the broken window-pane with Scotch tape and got a cloth and bucket and mopped up the pool of water on the floor. Then I ran across the short covered way to the cabins out back and went into mine, Number 9 on the right-hand side towards the lake, and took off my clothes and had a cold shower. My white Terylene shirt was smudged from my fall and I washed it and hung it up to dry.

I had already forgotten my chastisement by the storm and

the fact that I had behaved like a silly goose, and my heart was singing again with the prospect of my solitary evening and of being on my way the next day. On an impulse, I put on the best I had in my tiny wardrobe—my black velvet toreador pants with the rather indecent gold zip down the seat, itself most unchastely tight, and, not bothering with a bra, my golden thread Camelot sweater with the wide floppy turtleneck. I admired myself in the mirror, decided to pull my sleeves up above the elbows, slipped my feet into my gold Ferragamo sandals, and did the quick dash back to the lobby. There was just one good drink left in the quart of Virginia Gentleman bourbon that had already lasted me two weeks, and I filled one of the best cut-glass tumblers with ice cubes and poured the bourbon over them, shaking the bottle to get out the last drop. Then I pulled the most comfortable armchair over from the reception side of the room to stand beside the radio, turned the radio up, lit a Parliament from the last five in my box, took a stiff pull at my drink, and curled myself into the armchair.

The commercial, all about cats and how they loved Pussyfoot Prime Liver Meal, lilted on against the steady roar of the rain, whose tone only altered when a particularly heavy gust of wind hurled the water like grapeshot at the windows and softly shook the building. Inside, it was just as I had visualized—weatherproof, cosy and gay and glittering with lights and chromium. WOKO announced forty minutes of 'Music To Kiss By' and suddenly there were the Ink Spots singing 'Someone's Rockin' my Dream Boat' and I was back on the River Thames and it was five summers ago and we were drifting down past Kings Eyot in a punt and there was Windsor Castle in the distance and Derek was paddling while I worked the portable. We only had ten records, but whenever it came to be the turn of the Ink Spots' LP and the record got to 'Dream Boat', Derek would always plead, 'Play it again, Viv,' and I would have to go down on my knees and find the place with the needle.

So now my eyes filled with tears—not because of Derek, but because of the sweet pain of boy and girl and sunshine and first love with its tunes and snapshots and letters 'Sealed With A Loving Kiss'. They were tears of sentiment for lost childhood, and of self-pity for the pain that had been its winding sheet, and I let two tears roll down my cheeks before I brushed them away and decided to have a short orgy of remembering.

My name is Vivienne Michel and, at the time I was sitting in the Dreamy Pines motel and remembering, I was twenty-three. I am five feet six, and I always thought I had a good figure until the English girls at Astor House told me my behind stuck out too much and that I must wear a tighter bra. My eyes, as I have said, are blue and my hair a dark brown with a natural wave and my ambition is one day to give it a lion's streak to make me look older and more dashing. I like my rather high cheekbones, although these same girls said they made me look 'foreign', but my nose is too small, and my mouth too big so that it often looks sexy when I don't want it to. I have a sanguine temperament which I like to think is romantically tinged with melancholy, but I am wayward and independent to an extent that worried the sisters at the convent and exasperated Miss Threadgold at Astor House. ('Women should be willows, Vivienne. It is for men to be oak and ash.')

I am French-Canadian. I was born just outside Quebec at a little place called Sainte Famille on the north coast of the Ile d'Orléans, a long island that lies like a huge sunken ship in the middle of the St Lawrence River where it approaches the Quebec Straits. I grew up in and beside this great river, with the result that my main hobbies are swimming and fishing and camping and other outdoor things. I can't remember much about my parents—except that I loved my father and got on badly with my mother—because when I was eight they were both killed in a wartime air crash coming in to land at Montreal on their way to a wedding. The courts made me a ward of my widowed aunt, Florence Toussaint, and she moved into our little house and brought me up. We got on all right, and today I almost love her, but she was a Protestant, while I had been brought up as a Catholic, and I became the victim of the religious tug of war that has always been the bane of priest-ridden Quebec, so nearly exactly divided between the faiths. The Catholics won the battle over my spiritual well-being, and I was educated in the Ursuline Convent until I was fifteen. The sisters were strict and the accent was very much on piety, with the result that I learned a great deal of religious history and rather obscure dogma which I would gladly have exchanged for subjects that would have fitted me to be something other than a nurse or a nun and, when in the end the atmosphere became so stifling to my spirit that I begged to be taken away, my aunt gladly rescued me from 'The Papists' and it was decided that, at the age of sixteen, I should go to England and be 'finished'. This caused something of a local hullabaloo. Not only are the Ursulines the centre of Catholic tradition in Quebec—the Convent proudly owns the skull of Montcalm: for two centuries there have never been less than nine sisters kneeling at prayer, night and day, before the chapel altar—but my family had belonged to the very innermost citadel of French-Canadianism and that their daughter should flout both treasured folkways at one blow was a nine days' wonder—and scandal.

The true sons and daughters of Quebec form a society, almost a secret society, that must be as powerful as the Calvinist clique of Geneva, and the initiates refer to themselves proudly, male or female, as 'Canadiennes'. Lower, much lower, down the scale come the 'Canadiens'—Protestant Canadians. Then 'Les Anglais', which embraces all more or less recent immigrants from Britain, and lastly, 'Les Américains', a term of contempt. The Canadiennes pride themselves on their spoken French, although it is a bastard patois full of two-hundred-year-old words which Frenchmen themselves don't understand and is larded with Frenchified English words—rather, I suppose, like the relationship of Afrikaans to the language of the Dutch. The snobbery and exclusiveness of this Quebec clique extend even towards the French who live in France. These mother-people to the Canadiennes are referred to simply as 'Etrangers'! I have told all this at some length to explain that the defection from The Faith of a Michel from Sainte Famille was almost as heinous a crime as a defection, if that were possible, from the Mafia in Sicily, and it was made pretty plain to me that, in leaving the Ursulines and Quebec, I had just about burned my bridges so far as my spiritual guardians and my home town were concerned.

My aunt sensibly pooh-poohed my nerves over the social ostracism that followed—most of my friends were forbidden to have anything to do with me—but the fact remains that I arrived in England loaded with a sense of guilt and 'difference' that, added to my 'colonialism', were dreadful psychological burdens with which to face a smart finishing school for young ladies.

Miss Threadgold's Astor House was, like most of these very English establishments, in the Sunningdale area—a large Victorian stockbrokery kind of place, whose upper floors had been divided up with plasterboard to make bedrooms for twenty-five pairs of girls. Being a 'foreigner' I was teamed up with the other foreigner, a dusky Lebanese millionairess with huge tufts of mouse-coloured hair in her armpits, and an equal passion for chocolate fudge and an Egyptian film star called

Ben Saïd, whose gleaming photograph—gleaming teeth, moustache, eyes and hair—was soon to be torn up and flushed down the lavatory by the three senior girls of Rose Dormitory, of which we were both members. Actually I was saved by the Lebanese. She was so dreadful, petulant, smelly and obsessed with her money that most of the school took pity on me and went out of their way to be kind. But there were many others who didn't, and I was made to suffer agonies for my accent, my table manners, which were considered uncouth, my total lack of savoir-faire and, in general, for being a Canadian. I was also, I see now, much too sensitive and quick-tempered. I just wouldn't take the bullying and teasing, and when I had roughed up two or three of my tormentors, others got together with them and set upon me in bed one night and punched and pinched and soaked me with water until I burst into tears and promised I wouldn't 'fight like an elk' any more. After that, I gradually settled down, made an armistice with the place, and morosely set about learning to be a 'lady'.

It was the holidays that made up for everything. I made friends with a Scottish girl, Susan Duff, who liked the same open-air things as I did. She too was an only child and her parents were glad to have me to keep her company. So there was Scotland in the summer and skiing in the winter and spring—all over Europe, in Switzerland, Austria, Italy—and we stuck to each other through the finishing school and at the end we even 'came out' together and Aunt Florence produced five hundred pounds as my contribution to an idiotic joint dance at the Hyde Park Hotel, and I got on the same 'list' and went the rounds of similar idiotic dances at which the young men seemed to me rude and spotty and totally unmasculine compared with the young Canadians I had known. (But I may have been wrong because one of the spottiest of them rode in the Grand National that year and finished the course!)

And then I met Derek.

By now I was seventeen and a half and Susan and I were living in a tiny three-room flat in Old Church Street, just off the King's Road. It was the end of June and there wasn't much more of our famous 'season' to go and we decided to give a party for the few people we had met and actually liked. The family across the landing were going abroad on holiday, and they said we could have their flat in exchange for keeping an eye on it while they were away. We were both of us just about broke with 'keeping up with the Joneses' at all these balls, and I cabled Aunt Florence and got a hundred pounds out of her and Susan scraped up fifty and we decided to do it really well. We were going to ask about thirty people and we guessed that only twenty would come. We bought eighteen bottles of champagne—pink because it sounded more exciting—a ten-pound tin of caviar, two rather cheap tins of *foie gras* that looked all right when it was sliced up, and lots of garlicky things from Soho. We made a lot of brown bread-and-butter sandwiches with watercress and smoked salmon, and added some sort of Christmasy things like Elvas plums and chocolates—a stupid idea: no one ate any of them—and, by the time we had spread the whole lot out on a door taken off its hinges and covered with a gleaming table-cloth to make it seem like a buffet, it looked like a real grown-up feast.

The party was a great success, almost too much of a success. All the thirty came and some of them brought others and there was a real squash with people sitting on the stairs and even one man on the loo with a girl on his lap. The noise and the heat were terrific. Perhaps after all we weren't such squares as we had thought, or perhaps people really like squares so long as they are true squares and don't pretend. Anyway of course the worst happened and we ran out of drink! I was standing by the table when some wag drained the last bottle of champagne and shouted in a strangled voice, 'Water! Water! Or we'll never see England again.' I got fussed and said stupidly, 'Well, there just isn't any more,' when a tall young man standing against the wall said, 'Of course there is. You've forgotten the cellar,' and he took me by the elbow and shoved me out of the room and down the stairs. 'Come on,' he said firmly. 'Can't spoil a good party. We'll get some more from the pub.'

Well, we went to the pub and got two bottles of gin and an armful of bitter lemon and he insisted on paying for the gin so I paid for the lemon. He was rather tight in a pleasant way and explained that he'd been to another party before ours and that he'd been brought by a young married couple called Norman, who were friends of Susan's. He said his name was Derek Mallaby, but I didn't pay much attention as I was so anxious to get the drink back to the party. There were cheers as we came back up the stairs, but in fact the party had passed its peak and from then on people drifted away until there was nothing left but the usual hard core of particular friends, and characters who had nowhere to go for dinner. Then they too slowly broke up, including the Normans, who looked very nice and told Derek Mallaby that he would find the key under the mat, and Susan was suggesting that we go to the Popotte across the way, a place I didn't care for, when Derek Mallaby came and lifted my hair away from my ear and whispered rather hoarsely into it would I go slumming with him? So I said yes, largely I think because he was tall and because he had taken charge when I was stuck.

So we drifted out into the hot evening street leaving the dreadful battlefield of the party behind, and Susan and her friends wandered off and we got a taxi in the King's Road. Derek took me right across London to a spaghetti house called 'The Bamboo' near the Tottenham Court Road and we had spaghetti Bolognese and a bottle of instant-Beaujolais, as he called it, that he sent out for. He drank most of the Beaujolais, and told me that he lived not far from Windsor and that he was nearly eighteen and this was his last term at school and he was in the cricket eleven and that he had been given twenty-four hours off in London to see lawyers as his aunt had died and left him some money. His parents had spent the day with him and they had gone to see the MCC play Kent at Lords. They had then gone back to Windsor and left him with the Normans. He was supposed to have gone to a play and then home to bed, but there had been this other party and then mine, and now how about going on to the '400'?

Of course, I was thrilled. The '400' is the top nightclub in London and I had never graduated higher than the cellar places in Chelsea. I told him a bit about myself and made Astor House sound funny and he was very easy to talk to, and when the bill came he knew exactly how much to tip and it seemed to me that he was very grown-up to be still at school, but then English public schools are supposed to grow people up very quickly and teach them how to behave. He held my hand in the taxi, and that seemed to be all right, and they seemed to know him at the '400' and it was deliciously dark and he ordered gins and tonics and they put a half bottle of gin on the table that was apparently his from the last time he had been there. Maurice Smart's band was as smooth as cream and when we danced we fitted at once and his jive was just about the same as mine and I was really having fun. I began to notice the way his dark hair grew at the temples and that he had good hands and that he smiled not just at one's face but into one's eyes. We stayed there until four in the morning and the gin was finished and when we went out on to the pavement I had to hold on to him. He got a taxi and it seemed natural when he took me in his arms, and when he kissed me I kissed back. After I had twice taken his hand off my breast, the third time it seemed prissy not to leave it there, but when he moved it down and tried to put it up my skirt, I wouldn't let him, and when he took my hand and tried to put it on him I wouldn't do that either, although my whole body was hot with wanting these things. But then, thank heavens, we were outside the flat and he got out and took me to the door and we said we would see each other again and he would write. When we kissed goodbye, he put his hand down behind my back and squeezed my behind hard, and when his taxi disappeared round the corner I could still feel his hand there and I crept up to bed and looked into the mirror over the washbasin and my eyes and face were radiant as if they were lit up from inside and, although probably most of the lighting-up came from the gin, I thought, 'Oh, my heavens! I'm in love!'

3 / *SPRING'S AWAKENING*

It takes a long time to write these things, but only minutes to remember them, and when I came out of my daydream in the motel armchair WOKO was still playing 'Music To Kiss By' and it was someone who may have been Don Shirley improvising through 'Ain't She Sweet'. The ice in my drink had dissolved. I got up and put in some more from the icebox and I went back and curled up in my chair and drank a careful mouthful of the bourbon to make it last and lit another cigarette, and at once I was back again in that endless summer.

Derek's last term came to an end and we had exchanged four letters each. His first one had begun 'Dearest' and ended with love and kisses, and I had compromised with 'Dear' and 'love'. His were mostly about how many runs he had made, and mine were about the dances I had been to and the films and plays I had seen. He was going to spend the summer at his home, and he was very excited about a second-hand MG his parents were going to give him and would I come out with him in it? Susan was surprised when I said that I wouldn't be coming up to Scotland and that I wanted to stay on in the flat at any rate for the time being. I hadn't told her the truth about Derek, and because I always got up earlier than her, she didn't know about his letters. It wasn't like me to be secretive, but I treasured my 'love-affair' as I described it to myself, and it seemed to be so fragile and probably full of disappointments that I thought even to talk about it might bring it bad luck. For all I knew I might be just one in a whole row of Derek's girls. He was so attractive and grand, at any rate at school, that I imagined a long queue of 'Mayfair' sisters, all in organdie and all with titles, at his beck and call. So I simply said that I wanted to look around for a job and perhaps I would come up later, and in due course Susan went north and a fifth letter came from Derek saying would I come down next Saturday on the twelve o'clock from Paddington and he would meet me with the car at Windsor station?

And so began our regular and delicious routine. The first day he met me on the platform. We were rather shy, but he was so excited about his car that he quickly hurried me out to see it. It was wonderful—black with red leather upholstery and red wire wheels and all sorts of racing gimmicks like a strap round the bonnet and an outsize filler cap on the gas tank and the badge of the BRDC. We climbed in and I tied Derek's coloured silk handkerchief round my hair and the exhaust made a wonderful sexy noise as we accelerated across the High Street lights and turned up along the river. That day he took me as far as Bray, to show off the car, and we tore through the lanes with Derek doing quite unnecessary racing changes on the flattest curves. Sitting so near the ground, even at fifty one felt as if one was doing at least a hundred, and to begin with I clutched on to the safety grip on the dashboard and hoped for the best. But Derek was a good driver and I soon got confidence in him and controlled my trembles. He took me to a fearfully smart place, the Hotel de Paris, and we had smoked salmon, which cost extra, and roast chicken and ice cream and then he hired an electric canoe from the boat-house next door and we chugged sedately up-river and under Maidenhead Bridge and found a little backwater, just this side of

Cookham Lock, where Derek rammed the canoe far in under the branches. He had brought a portable gramophone with him and I scrambled down to his end of the canoe and we sat and later lay side by side and listened to the records and watched a small bird hopping about in the network of branches over our heads. It was a beautiful, drowsy afternoon and we kissed but didn't go any further and I felt reassured that Derek didn't after all think I was 'easy'. Later the midges came and we nearly upset the canoe trying to get it out of the creek backwards, but then we were going fast down-river with the current and there were a lot of other boats with couples and families in them, but I was quite certain we looked the gayest and handsomest of everyone. We drove back and went down to Eton and had scrambled eggs and coffee in a place called The Thatched House that Derek knew about and then he suggested we should go to the cinema.

The Royalty Kinema was on Farquhar Street, one of the small streets leading down from the Castle towards the Ascot road. It was a meagre-looking place, showing two Westerns, a cartoon and so-called 'News' that consisted of what the Queen had been doing a month ago. I realized why Derek had chosen it when he paid twelve shillings for a box. There was one on each side of the projection room, about six feet square, dark and with two chairs, and as soon as we went in Derek pulled his chair close to me and began kissing and feeling me. At first I thought, Oh, God! Is this where he brings them? But after a bit I sort of melted and then his hands were slowly exploring me and they were gentle and seemed to know, and then they were there and I hid my face against his shoulder and bit my lip with the exquisite tingle and then it was all over and I was flooded with warmth and tears came by themselves out of my eyes and wet the collar of his shirt.

He kissed me gently and whispered that he loved me and

that I was the most wonderful girl in the world. But I sat up and away from him and dabbed at my eyes and tried to watch the film and reflected that I had lost my virginity, or some kind of virginity, and that now he would never respect me again. But then the interval came and he bought me an ice and put his arm round the back of my chair and whispered that it was being the most wonderful day of his life and that we must have the same day over and over again. And I told myself not to be silly. That this was just petting. Everybody did it, and anyway it had been rather marvellous and it wasn't as if I would get a baby or anything. Besides, boys wanted to pet and if I didn't do it with him he would find some other girl who would. So when the lights went out again and his hands came back it seemed natural that they should go to my breasts and that excited me. Then his breath came panting against my neck and he said, 'Oh, Baby!' in a long-drawn-out kind of sigh and I felt a sort of pang of excitement as if some kind of barrier had disappeared from between us and I felt motherly towards him and kissed him and from that moment on we were somehow different kinds of friends.

He drove me back to catch the last train for London and we arranged to meet at the same time on the next Saturday and he stood and waved for as long as I could see him under the yellow lights of that darling little station and so our real love-affair began. It was always the same, with perhaps different places for luncheon and high tea, the river, the gramophone, the little box in the cinema, but now there was added the extra thrill of the physical side and always, in the boat, the car, the cinema, our hands were on each other's bodies, more lingering, more expert as the endless summer drew on into September.

In my memory of those days the sun is always shining and the willows dip into water as limpid clear as the sky. Swans ride in the shadows of the poplars and swallows dip and skim as the Thames slips down from Queens Eyot, past Boveney Lock and Coocoo Weir, where we used to bathe, and on down the long stretch through Brocas meadows towards Windsor Bridge. It surely must have rained, there must have been noisy holiday-makers crowding our river, there must have been clouds in our private skies, but if there were I can't remember them. The weeks slipped by like the river, sparkling, luminous, full of enchantment.

And then came the last Saturday of September and, though till then we had ignored the fact, a new chapter had to be opened. Susan was coming back to the flat on Monday, I had the chance of a job, and Derek was going up to Oxford. We pretended it would all be the same. I would explain to Susan and there would be weekends when I could go to Oxford or Derek come up to London. We didn't discuss our affair. It was obvious that it would go on. Derek had talked vaguely of my meeting his parents, but he had never pressed it and on our Saturdays together there were always so many better things to do. Perhaps I thought it rather odd that Derek seemed to have no time for me during the week, but he played a lot of cricket and tennis and had hosts of friends all of whom he said were a bore. I didn't want to get mixed up in this side of his life, at any rate not for the present. I was happy to have him absolutely to myself for our one day a week. I didn't want to share him with a crowd of other people who would anyway make me shy. So things were left very much in the air, and I just didn't look beyond the next Saturday.

That day Derek was particularly affectionate and in the evening he took me to the Bridge Hotel and we had three rounds of gins and tonics, though usually we hardly drank at all. And then he insisted on champagne for dinner and by the time we got to our little cinema we were both rather tight. I was glad, because it would make me forget that tomorrow would mean the turning of a new page and the breaking up of all our darling routines. But when we got into our little box, Derek was morose. He didn't take me in his arms as usual but sat a little away from me and smoked and watched the film. I came close to him and took his hand, but he just sat and looked straight in front of him. I asked him what was the matter. After a moment he said obstinately, 'I want to sleep with you. Properly, I mean.'

I was shocked. It was his rough tone of voice. We had talked about it of course, but it was always agreed, more or less, that this would come 'later'. Now I used the same old arguments, but I was nervous and upset. Why did he have to spoil our last evening? He argued back, fiercely. I was being a hard-boiled virgin. It was bad for him. Anyway, we were lovers, so why not behave like lovers? I said I was frightened of getting a baby. He said that was easy. There were things he could wear. But why now? I argued. We couldn't do it here. Oh yes we could. There was plenty of room. And he wanted to do it before he went up to Oxford. It would sort of, sort of marry us.

Tremulously I considered this. Perhaps there was something in it. It would be a kind of seal on our love. But I was frightened. Hesitantly I said had he got one of these 'things'? He said no, but there was an all-night chemist and he would go and buy one. And he kissed me and got up eagerly and walked out of the box.

I sat and stared dully at the screen. Now I couldn't refuse him! He would come back and it would be messy and horrible in this filthy little box in this filthy little back-street cinema and it was going to hurt and he would despise me afterwards for giving in. I had an instinct to get up and run out and down to the station and take the next train back to London. But that would make him furious. It would hurt his vanity.

I wouldn't be being 'a sport', and the rhythm of our friendship, so much based on us both 'having fun', would be wrecked. And, after all, was it fair on him to hold this back from him? Perhaps it really was bad for him not to be able to do it properly. And, after all, it had to happen some time. One couldn't choose the perfect moment for that particular thing. No girl ever seemed to enjoy the first time. Perhaps it would be better to get it over with. Anything not to make him angry! Anything better than the danger of wrecking our love!

The door opened and there was a brief shaft of light from the lobby. Then he was beside me, breathless and excited. 'I've got it,' he whispered. 'It was terribly embarrassing. There was a girl behind the counter. I didn't know what to call it. I finally said, "One of those things for not having babies. You know." She was cool as a cucumber. She asked me what quality. I said the best of course. I almost thought she was going to ask "What size?"' He laughed and held me tight. I giggled feebly back. Better to 'be a sport'! Better not to make a drama out of it! Nowadays nobody did. It would make it all so embarrassing, particularly for him.

His preliminary love-making was so perfunctory it almost made me cry. Then he pushed his chair to the back of the box and took off his coat and laid it down on the wooden floor. When he told me to, I lay down on it and he knelt beside me. He said to put my feet up against the front of the box and I did, and I was so cramped and uncomfortable that I said, 'No, Derek! Please! Not here!' But then he was somehow on top of me in a dreadful clumsy embrace and all my instinct was somehow to help him so that at least he would have pleasure from it and not be angry with me afterwards.

And then the world fell in!

There was suddenly a great gush of yellow light and a furious voice said from above and behind me, 'What the hell do you think you're doing in my cinema? Get up, you filthy little swine.'

I don't know why I didn't faint. Derek was standing, his face white as a sheet. I scrambled to my feet, banging against the wall of the box. I stood there, waiting to be killed, waiting to be shot dead.

The black silhouette in the doorway pointed at my bag on the floor with the white scrap of my pants beside it. 'Pick those up.' I bent down quickly as if I had been hit and clutched the pants into a ball in my hand to try and hide them. 'Now get out!' He stood there half blocking the entrance, while we shambled past him, broken people.

The manager banged the door of the box shut and got in front of us, thinking, I suppose, that we might make a run for it. Two or three people had seeped out of the back seats into the foyer. (The whole audience must have heard the manager's voice. Had the seats below us heard the whole thing, the argument, the pause, then Derek's instructions what to do? I shuddered.) The ticket woman had come out of her box and one or two passersby, who had been examining the programme, gazed in from under the cheap coloured lights over the entrance.

The manager was a plump, dark man with a tight suit and a flower in his buttonhole. His face was red with rage as he looked us up and down. 'Filthy little brats!' He turned on me. 'And I've seen you here before. You're nothing better than a common prostitute. I've a damned good mind to call the police. Indecent exposure. Disturbing the peace.' He ran the heavy words easily off his tongue. He must have used them often before in his sleazy little house of private darkness. 'Names, please.' He took a notebook out of his pocket and licked a stub of pencil. He was looking at Derek. Derek stammered, 'Er, James Grant' (the film had starred Cary Grant). 'Er,

24 Acacia Road, Nettlebed.' The manager looked up, 'There aren't any roads in Nettlebed. Only the Henley—Oxford road.' Derek said obstinately, 'Yes, there are. At the back,' he added weakly. 'Sort of lanes.' 'And you?' he turned towards me, suspiciously. My mouth was dry. I swallowed. 'Miss Thompson, Audrey Thompson. 24' (I realized it was the same number that Derek had chosen, but I couldn't think of another) 'Thomas' (I almost said Thompson again!) 'Road. London.' 'District?' I didn't know what he meant. I gaped hopelessly at him. 'Postal district,' he said impatiently. I remembered Chelsea. 'S.W.6,' I said weakly. The manager snapped his book shut. 'All right. Get out of here both of you.' He pointed out into the street. We edged nervously past him and he followed us, still pointing. 'And don't ever come back to my establishment again! I know you both! You ever show up again, I'll have the police on you!'

The small host of sneering, accusing eyes followed us. I took Derek's arm (why didn't he take mine?) and we went out under the hideous bright lights and turned by instinct to the right and down the hill so that we could walk faster. We didn't stop until we got to a side street and we went in there and slowly started to work our way back to where the MG was parked up the hill from the cinema.

Derek didn't say a word until we were getting close to the car. Then he said, matter-of-factly, 'Mustn't let them get the number. I'll go and get her, and pick you up opposite Fullers on Windsor Hill. 'Bout ten minutes.' Then he freed himself from my arm and went off up the street.

I stood and watched him go, the tall, elegant figure that was once more proud and upright, and then I turned and went back to where a lane led up parallel with Farquhar Street towards the Castle.

I found that I still had my pants crushed in my hand. I put

them in my bag. The open bag made me think of my appearance. I stopped under a street-light and took out my mirror. I looked dreadful. My face was so white it was almost green, and my eyes belonged to a hunted animal. My hair stuck up at the back where it had been rumpled by the floor and my mouth was smeared by Derek's kisses. I shuddered. 'Filthy little swine!' How right! All of me felt unclean, degraded, sinful. What would happen to us? Would the man check on the addresses and put the police on us? Someone would certainly remember us from today or from other Saturdays. Someone would remember the number of Derek's car, some little boy who collected car numbers. There was always some Nosey Parker at the scene of a crime. Crime? Yes, of course it was, one of the worst in puritan England—sex, nakedness, indecent exposure. I imagined what the manager must have seen when Derek got up from me. Ugh! I shivered with disgust. But now Derek would be waiting for me. My hands had automatically been tidying my face. I gave it a last look. It was the best I could do. I hurried on up the street and turned down Windsor Hill, hugging the wall, expecting people to turn and point. 'There she goes!' 'That's her!' 'Filthy little swine!'

4 / 'DEAR VIV'

That summer's night hadn't finished with me. Opposite Fullers, a policeman was standing by Derek's car, arguing with him. Derek turned and saw me. 'Here she is, officer. I said she wouldn't be a minute. Had to, er, powder her nose. Didn't you, darling?'

More trouble! More lies! I said yes, breathlessly, and climbed into the seat beside Derek. The policeman grinned slyly at me, and said to Derek, 'All right, sir. But another time remember there's no parking on the Hill. Even for an emergency like that.' He fingered his moustache. Derek put the car in gear, thanked the policeman and gave him the wink of a dirty joke shared, and we were off at last.

Derek said nothing until we had turned right at the lights at the bottom. I thought he was going to drop me at the station, but he continued on along the Datchet road. 'Phew!' He let the air out of his lungs with relief. 'That was a close shave! Thought we were for it. Nice thing for my parents to read in the paper tomorrow. And Oxford! I should have had it.'

'It was ghastly.'

There was so much feeling in my voice that he looked sideways at me. 'Oh, well. The path of true love and all that.' His voice was light and easy. He had recovered. When would I? 'Damned shame really,' he went on casually. 'Just when we'd got it all set up.' He put enthusiasm into his voice to carry me with him. 'Tell you what. There's an hour before the train. Why don't we walk up along the river. It's a well-known beat for Windsor couples. Absolutely private. Pity to waste everything, time and so on, now we've made up our minds.'

The 'so on', I thought, meant 'the thing' he had bought. I was aghast. I said urgently, 'Oh, but I can't, Derek! I simply can't! You've no idea how awful I feel about what happened.'

He looked quickly at me. 'What do you mean, awful? You feeling ill or something?'

'Oh, it's not that. It's just that, that it was all so horrible. So shaming.'

'Oh, that!' His voice was contemptuous. 'We got away with it, didn't we? Come on. Be a sport!'

That again! But I did want to be comforted, feel his arms round me, be certain he still loved me, although everything had gone so wrong for him. But my legs began to tremble at the thought of going through it all again. I clutched my knees with my hands to control them. I said weakly, 'Oh, well . . .'

'That's my girl!'

We went over the bridge and Derek pulled the car in to the side. He helped me over a stile into a field and put his arm round me and guided me along the little towpath past some house-boats moored under the willows. 'Wish we had one of those,' he said. 'How about breaking into one? Lovely double bed. Probably some drink in the cupboards.'

'Oh, no, Derek! For heaven's sake! There's been enough trouble.' I could imagine the loud voice. 'What's going on in there? Are you the owners of this boat? Come on out and let's have a look at you.'

Derek laughed. 'Perhaps you're right. Anyway the grass is just as soft. Aren't you excited? You'll see. It's wonderful. Then we'll really be lovers.'

'Oh, yes, Derek. But you will be gentle, won't you? I shan't be any good at it the first time.'

Derek squeezed me excitedly. 'Don't you worry. I'll show you.'

I was feeling better, stronger. It was lovely walking with him in the moonlight. But there was a grove of trees ahead and I looked at it fearfully. I knew that would be where it was going to happen. I must, I must make it easy and good for him! I mustn't be silly! I mustn't cry!

The path led through the grove. Derek looked about him. 'In there,' he said. 'I'll go first. Keep your head down.'

We crept in among the branches. Sure enough, there was a little clearing. Other people had been there before. There was a cigarette packet, a Coca-Cola bottle. The moss and leaves had been beaten down. I had the feeling that this was a brothel bed where hundreds, perhaps thousands, of lovers had pressed and struggled. But now there was no turning back. At least it must be a good place for it if so many others had used it.

Derek was eager, impatient. He put his coat down for me and at once started, almost feverishly, his hands devouring me. I tried to melt, but my body was still cramped with nerves and my limbs felt like wood. I wished he would say something, something sweet and loving, but he was intent and purposeful, manhandling me almost brutally, treating me as if I was a big clumsy doll. 'Only a Paper Doll, for Me to Call My Own'—the Ink Spots again! I could hear the deep bass of 'Hoppy' Jones and the sweet soprano counterpoint of Bill Kenny, so piercingly sweet that it tore at the heart-strings. And underneath, the deep pulse-beat of Charlie Fuqua's guitar. The tears squeezed out of my eyes. Oh, God, what was happening to me? And then the sharp pain and the short scream I quickly stifled and he was lying on top of me, his chest heaving and his heart beating heavily against my breast. I put my arms round him and felt his shirt wet against my hands.

We lay like that for long minutes. I watched the moonlight filtering down through the branches, and tried to stop my tears. So that was it! The great moment. A moment I would never have again. So now I was a woman and the girl was gone! And there had been no pleasure, only pain like they all said. But there remained something. This man in my arms. I held him more tightly to me. I was his now, entirely his, and he was mine. He would look after me. We belonged. Now I would never be alone again. There were two of us.

Derek kissed my wet cheek and scrambled to his feet. He held out his hands and I pulled down my skirt and he hauled me up. He looked into my face and there was embarrassment in his half-smile. 'I hope it didn't hurt too much.'

'No. But was it all right for you?'

'Oh, yes, rather.'

He bent down and picked up his coat. He looked at his watch. 'I say! Only a quarter of an hour for the train! We'd better get moving.'

We scrambled back on to the path and as we walked along I pulled a comb through my hair and brushed at my skirt. Derek walked silently beside me. His face under the moon was now closed, and when I put my arm through his there was no answering pressure. I wished he would be loving, talk about our next meeting, but I could feel that he was suddenly withdrawn, cold. I hadn't got used to men's faces after they've done it. I blamed myself. It hadn't been good enough. And I had cried. I had spoiled it for him.

We came to the car, and drove silently to the station. I stopped him at the entrance. Under the yellow light his face was taut and strained and his eyes only half met mine. I said, 'Don't come to the train, darling. I can find my way. What about next Saturday? I could come down to Oxford. Or would you rather wait until you're settled in?'

He said defensively. 'Trouble is, Viv. Things are going to be different at Oxford. I'll have to see. Write to you.'

I tried to read his face. This was so different from our usual parting. Perhaps he was tired. God knew I was! I said, 'Yes, of course. But write to me quickly, darling. I'd like to know how you're getting on.' I reached up and kissed him on the lips. His own lips hardly responded.

He nodded. 'Well, so long, Viv,' and with a kind of twisted smile he turned and went off round the corner to his car.

It was two weeks later that I got the letter. I had written twice, but there had been no answer. In desperation I had even telephoned, but the man at the other end had gone away and come back and said that Mr Mallaby wasn't at home.

The letter began, 'Dear Viv, This is going to be a difficult letter to write.' When I had got that far I went into my bedroom and locked the door and sat on my bed and gathered my courage. The letter went on to say that it had been a wonderful summer and he would never forget me. But now his life had changed and he would have a lot of work to do and there wouldn't be much room for 'girls'. He had told his parents about me, but they disapproved of our 'affair'. They said it wasn't fair to go on with a girl if one wasn't going to marry her. 'They are terribly insular, I'm afraid, and they have ridiculous ideas about "foreigners", although heaven knows I regard you as just like any other English girl and you know I adore your accent.' They were set on his marrying the daughter of some neighbour in the country. 'I've never told you about this, which I'm afraid was very naughty of me, but as a matter of fact we're sort of semi-engaged. We had such a marvellous time together and you were such a sport that I didn't want to spoil it all.' He said he hoped very much we would 'run into each other' again one day and in the meantime he had asked Fortnum's to send me a dozen bottles of pink champagne, 'the best', to remind me of the first time we had met. 'And I do hope this letter won't upset you too much, Viv, as I really think you're the most wonderful girl, far too good for someone like me. With much love, happy memories, Derek.'

Well, it took just ten minutes to break my heart and about another six months to mend it. Accounts of other people's aches and pains are uninteresting because they are so similar to everybody else's, so I won't go into details. I didn't even tell Susan. As I saw it, I'd behaved like a tramp, from the very first evening, and I'd been treated like a tramp. In this tight little world of England, I was a Canadian, and therefore a foreigner, an outsider—fair game. The fact that I hadn't seen it happening to me was more fool me. Born yesterday! Better get wise, or you'll go on being hurt! But beneath this open-eyed, chin-up rationalization, the girl in me whimpered and cringed, and for a time I cried at night and went down on my knees to the Holy Mother I had forsaken and prayed that She would give Derek back to me. But of course She wouldn't, and my pride forbade me to plead with him or to follow up my curt little note of acknowledgement to his letter and the return of the champagne to Fortnum's. The endless summer had ended. All that was left were some poignant Ink Spot memories, and the imprint of the nightmare in the cinema in Windsor, the marks of which I knew I would bear all my life.

I was lucky. The job I had been trying for came up. It was through the usual friend-of-a-friend, and it was on the *Chelsea Clarion*, a glorified parish magazine that had gone in for small ads and had established itself as a kind of market-place for people looking for flats and rooms and servants in the southwest part of London. It had added some editorial pages that dealt only with local problems—the hideous new lamp standards, infrequent buses on the Number 11 route, the theft of milk bottles—things that really affected the local housewives, and it ran a whole page of local gossip, mostly 'Chelsea', that 'everybody' came to read and that somehow managed to dodge libel actions. It also had a hard-hitting editorial on Empire Loyalist lines that exactly suited the politics of the neighbourhood, and, for good measure, it was stylishly made up each week (it was a weekly) by a man called Harling who was quite a dab at getting the most out of the old-fashioned type faces that were all our steam-age jobbing printers in Pimlico had in stock. In fact it was quite a good little paper, and the staff liked it so much they worked for a pittance and even for nothing when the ads didn't materialize in times like August and over the holidays. I got five pounds a week (we were non-union: not important enough), plus commission on any ads I could rustle up.

So I quietly tucked the fragments of my heart somewhere under my ribs and decided to get along without one for the future. I would rely on brains and guts and shoe-leather to show these damned English snobs that if I couldn't get anywhere else with them I could at least make a living out of them. So I went to work by day and cried by night and I became the most willing horse on the paper. I made tea for the staff, attended the funerals and got the lists of the mourners right, wrote spiky paragraphs for the gossip page, ran the competition column, and even checked the clues of the crossword before it went into type. And, in between, I hustled round the neighbourhood, charming ads out of the most hardbitten shops and hotels and restaurants and piling up my twenty-per-cents with the tough old Scotswoman who kept the accounts. Soon I was making good money—twelve to twenty pounds a week—and the editor thought he would economize by stabilizing me at a salary of fifteen, so he installed me in a cubby-hole next to him and I became his editorial assistant, which apparently carried with it the privilege of sleeping with him. But at the first pinch of my behind I told him that I was engaged to a man in Canada, and, when I said it, I looked him so furiously in the eye that he got the message and left me alone. I liked him and from then on we got on fine. He was an ex-Beaverbrook reporter called Len Holbrook, who had come into some money and had decided to go into business for himself. He was a Welshman and, like all of them, something of an idealist. He had decided that if he couldn't change the world he would at least make a start on Chelsea, and he bought the broken-down *Clarion* and started laying about him. He had a tip-off on the Council and another in the local Labour Party organization, and he got off to a flying start when he revealed that a jerry-builder had got the contract for a new block of Council flats and that he wasn't building to specification—not putting enough steel in the concrete or something. The Nationals picked up the story, with tongs because it stank of libel, and, as luck would have it, cracks began to appear in the uprights and pictures got taken. There was an inquiry, the builder lost his contract and his licence, and the *Clarion* put a red St-George-and-Dragon on its mast-head. There were other campaigns, like the ones I mentioned earlier, and suddenly people were reading the little paper and it put on more pages and soon had a circulation of around forty thousand and the Nationals were regularly stealing its stories and giving it an occasional puff in exchange.

Well, I settled down in my new job as 'Assistant to the Editor' and I was given more writing to do and less legwork and in due course, after I had been there for a year, I graduated to a by-line and 'Vivienne Michel' became a public person and my salary went up to twenty guineas. Len liked the way I got on with things and wasn't afraid of people, and he taught me a lot about writing—tricks like hooking the reader with your lead paragraph, using short sentences, avoiding 'okay' English and, above all, writing about *people*. This he had learned from the *Express*, and he was always drumming it into my head. For instance, he had a phobia about the 11 and 22 bus services and he was always chasing them. I began one of my many stories about them, 'Conductors on the Number 11 service complain that they have to work to too tight a schedule in the rush-hours.' Len put his pencil through it. 'People, people, people! This is how it ought to go, "Frank Donaldson, a wideawake young man of twenty-seven, has a wife, Gracie, and two children, Bill, six, and Emily, five. And he has a grouse. 'I haven't seen my kids in the evening ever since the summer holidays,' he told me in the neat little parlour of number 36 Bolton Lane. 'When I get home they're always in bed. You see, I'm a conductor, on the 11 route, and we've been running an hour late regular, ever since the new schedules came in.'"' Len stopped. 'See what I mean? There are people driving those buses. They're more interesting than the buses. Now you go out and find a Frank Donaldson and make that story of yours come alive.' Cheap stuff, I suppose, corny angles, but that's journalism and I was in the trade and I did what he told me and my copy began to draw the letters—from the Donaldsons of the neighbourhood and their wives and their mates. And editors seem to love letters. They make a paper look busy and read.

I stayed with the *Clarion* another two years, until I was just over twenty-one, and by then I was getting offers from the Nationals, from the *Express* and the *Mail*, and it seemed to me it was time to get out of SW3 and into the world. I was still living with Susan. She had got a job with the Foreign Office in something called 'Communications', about which she was very secretive, and she had a boy-friend from the same department and I knew it wouldn't be long before they got engaged and she would want the whole flat. My own private life was a vacuum—a business of drifting friendships and semi-flirtations from which I always recoiled, and I was in danger of becoming a hard, if successful, little career girl, smoking too many cigarettes and drinking too many vodkas-and-tonics and eating alone out of tins. My gods, or rather goddesses (Katherine Whitehorn and Penelope Gilliatt were outside my orbit), were Drusilla Beyfus, Veronica Papworth, Jean Campbell, Shirley Lord, Barbara Griggs and Anne Sharpley—the top women journalists—and I only wanted to be as good as any of them and nothing else in the world.

And then, at a press show in aid of a Baroque Festival in Munich, I met Kurt Rainer of the VWZ.

5 / A BIRD WITH A WING DOWN

The rain was still crashing down, its violence unchanged. The eight o'clock news continued its talk of havoc and disaster—a multiple crash on Route 9, railway tracks flooded at Schenectady, traffic at a standstill in Troy, heavy rain likely to continue for several hours. American life is completely dislocated by storms and snow and hurricanes. When American automobiles can't move, life comes to a halt, and, when their famous schedules can't be met, they panic and go into a kind of paroxysm of frustration, besieging railway stations, jamming the long-distance wires, keeping their radios permanently switched on for any crumb of comfort. I could imagine the chaos on the roads and in the cities, and I hugged my cosy solitude to me.

My drink was nearly dead. I kept it just alive with some more ice cubes, lit another cigarette, and settled down again in my chair while a disc jockey announced half an hour of Dixieland jazz.

Kurt hadn't liked jazz. He thought it decadent. He also stopped me smoking and drinking and using lipstick and life became a serious business of art galleries and concerts and lecture halls. As a contrast to my meaningless, rather empty life, it was a welcome change and I dare say the diet of Teutonism appealed to the rather heavy seriousness that underlies the Canadian character.

VWZ, the Verband Westdeutscher Zeitungen, was an independent news agency financed by a co-operative of West German newspapers rather on the lines of Reuters. Kurt Rainer was its first representative in London and when I met him he was on the look-out for an English Number two to read the papers and weeklies for items of German interest while he did the high-level diplomatic stuff and covered outside assignments. He took me out to dinner that night, to Schmidts in Charlotte Street, and was rather charmingly serious about the importance of his job and how much it might mean for Anglo-German relationships. He was a powerfully built, outdoor type of young man whose bright fair hair and candid blue eyes made him look younger than his thirty years. He told me that he came from Augsburg, near Munich, and that he was an only child of parents who were both doctors and had both been rescued from a concentration camp by the Americans. They had been informed on and arrested for listening to the Allied radio and for preventing young Kurt from joining the Hitler Youth Movement. He had been educated at Munich High School and at the University, and had then gone into journalism, graduating to *Die Welt*, the leading West German newspaper, from which he had been chosen for this London job because of his good English. He asked me what I did, and the next day I went round to his two-room office in Chancery Lane and showed him some of my work. With typical thoroughness he had already checked up on me through friends at the Press Club, and a week later I found myself installed in the room next to his with the PA/Reuter and the Exchange Telegraph tickers chattering beside my desk. My salary was wonderful—thirty pounds a week—and I soon got to love the work, particularly operating the Telex with our *Zentrale* in Hamburg, and the twice-daily rush to catch the morning and evening deadlines of the German papers. My lack of German was only a slight handicap, for, apart from Kurt's copy which he put over by telephone, all my stuff went over the Telex in English and was translated at the other end, and the Telex operators in Hamburg had enough English to chatter with me when I was on the machine. It was rather a mechanical job, but you had to be quick and accurate and it was fun judging the success or failure of what I sent by the German cuttings that came in a few days later. Soon Kurt had enough confidence to leave me alone in charge of the office, and there were exciting little emergencies I had to handle by myself with the thrill of knowing that twenty editors in Germany were depending on me to be fast and right. It all seemed so much more important and responsible than the parochial trivialities of the *Clarion*, and I enjoyed the authority of Kurt's directions and decisions, combined with the constant smell of urgency that goes with news agency work.

In due course Susan got married and I moved out to furnished rooms in Bloomsbury Square in the same building as Kurt. I had wondered if this was a good idea, but he was so *korrekt* and our relationship was so *kameradschaftlich*—words which he constantly employed about social situations—that I thought I was being at least adequately sensible. It was very silly of me. Apart from the fact that Kurt probably misunderstood my easy acceptance of his suggestion that I find a place in his building, it now became natural that we should walk home together from the near-by office. Dinners together became more frequent and, later, to spare the expense, he would bring his gramophone up to my sitting-room and I would cook something for both of us. Of course, I saw the danger and I invented several friends to spend the evening with. But this meant sitting by myself in some cinema after a lonely meal with all the nuisance of men trying to pick one up. And Kurt remained so *korrekt* and our relationship on such a straightforward and even highminded level that my apprehensions came to seem idiotic and more and more I accepted a comradely way of life that seemed not only totally respectable but also adult in the modern fashion. I was all the more confident because, after about three months of this peaceful existence, Kurt, on his return from a visit to Germany, told me that he had become engaged. She was a childhood friend called Trude and, from all he told me, they were ideally suited. She was the daughter of a Heidelberg professor of philosophy, and the placid eyes that stared out of the snapshots he showed me, and the gleaming braided hair and trim dirndl, were a living advertisement for '*Kinder, Kirche, Küche*'.

Kurt involved me closely in the whole affair, translating Trude's letters to me, discussing the number of children they would have, and asking my advice on the decoration of the flat they planned to buy in Hamburg when he had finished his three years' stint in London and had saved enough money for marriage. I became a sort of Universal Aunt to the two of them, and I would have found the role ridiculous if it hadn't all seemed quite natural and rather fun—like having two big dolls to play at 'Weddings' with. Kurt had even planned their sex life minutely and the details which he insisted, rather perversely, on sharing with me, were at first embarrassing and then, because he was so clinical about the whole subject, highly educative. On the honeymoon in Venice (all Germans go to Italy for their honeymoons) they would of course do it every night because, Kurt said, it was most important that 'the act' should be technically perfect and, to achieve this, much practice was necessary. To this end, they would have a light dinner, because a full stomach was not desirable, and they would retire not later than eleven o'clock because it was important to have at least eight hours' sleep 'to recharge the batteries'. Trude, he said, was unawakened and inclined to be 'kühl' sexually, while he was of a passionate temperament. So there would have to be much preliminary sex-play to bring the curve of her passion up to his. This would need restraint on his part, and in this matter he would have to be firm with himself, for as he told me, it was essential to a happy marriage that the climax should be reached simultaneously by the partners. Only thus could the thrilling summits of *Ekstase* become the equal property of both. After the honeymoon they would sleep together on Wednesdays and Saturdays. To do it more often would weaken his 'batteries' and might reduce his efficiency at the 'Büro'. All this Kurt illustrated with a wealth of most explicit scientific words and even with diagrams and drawings done on the table-cloth with a fork.

The lectures, for such they were, convinced me that Kurt was a lover of quite exceptional finesse, and I admit I was fascinated and rather envious of the well-regulated and thoroughly hygienic delights that were being prepared for Trude. There were many nights when I longed for these experiences to be mine, and for someone to play upon me also like, as Kurt put it, 'a great violinist playing upon his instrument'. And it was inevitable, I suppose, that in my dreams it was Kurt who came to me in that role—so safe, so gentle, so deeply understanding of a woman's physical needs.

The months passed and gradually the tone and frequency of Trude's letters began to change. It was I who noticed it first, but I said nothing. There were more frequent and sharper complaints about the length of the waiting period, the tender passages became more perfunctory, and the pleasures of a summer holiday on the Tegernsee, where Trude had met up with a 'happy group', after a first ecstatic description, were, significantly I thought, not mentioned again. And then, after three weeks of silence from Trude, Kurt came up to my rooms one evening, his face pale and wet with tears. I was lying on the sofa, reading, and he fell on his knees beside me and buried his head on my breast. It was all over, he said between sobs. She had met another man, at the Tegernsee of course, a doctor from Munich, a widower. He had proposed to her and she had accepted. It had been love at first sight. Kurt must understand that such a thing only happened once in a girl's lifetime. He must forgive her and forget her. She was not good enough for him. (Ah! That shabby phrase again!) They must remain honourable friends. The marriage was to take place next month. Kurt must try and wish her well. Farewell, your abject Trude.

Kurt's arms were round me and he was holding me desperately. 'Now I have only you,' he said through his sobs. 'You must be kind. You must give me comfort.'

I smoothed his hair as maternally as I could, wondering how to escape from his embrace, yet at the same time being melted by the despair of this strong man and by his dependence on me. I tried to make my voice sound matter-of-fact. 'Well, if you ask me, it was a lucky escape. Any girl as changeable as that would not have made you a good wife. There are many other better girls in Germany. Come on, Kurt.' I struggled to sit up. 'We'll go out to dinner and a cinema. It will take your mind off things. It's no good crying over spilt milk. Come on!' I freed myself rather breathlessly and we both got to our feet.

Kurt hung his head. 'Ah, but you are good to me, Viv. You are a real friend in need—*eine echte Kameradin*. And you are right. I must not behave like a weakling. You will be ashamed of me. And that I could not bear.' He gave me a tortured smile and went to the door and let himself out.

Only two weeks later we were lovers. It was somehow inevitable. I had half known it would be, and I did nothing to dodge my fate. I was not in love with him, and yet we had grown so close in so many other ways that the next step of sleeping together was bound, inexorably, to follow. The details were really quite dull. The occasional friendly kiss on the cheek, as if to a sister, came by degrees closer to my mouth and one day was on it. There was a pause in the campaign while I came to take this kind of kiss for granted, then came the soft assault on my breasts and then on my body, all so pleasurable, so calm, so lacking in drama, and then, one evening in my sitting-room, the slow stripping of my body 'because I must see how beautiful you are', the feeble, almost languorous protests, and then the scientific operation that had been prepared for Trude. And how delicious it was, in the wonderful privacy of my own room! How safe, how unhurried, how reassuring the precautions! And how strong and gentle Kurt was, and of all things to associate with love-making, how divinely polite! A single flower after each time, the room tidied after each passionate ecstasy, studious correctness in the office and before other people, never a rough or even a dirty word—it was like a series of exquisite operations by a surgeon with the best bedside manners in the world. Of course, it was all rather impersonal. But I liked that. It was sex without involvement or danger, a delicious heightening of the day's routine which each time left me sleek and glowing like a pampered cat.

I might have realized, or at any rate guessed, that, at least among amateur women as opposed to prostitutes, there is no physical love without emotional involvement—over a long period, that is. Physical intimacy is halfway to love, and enslavement is much of the other half. Admittedly my mind and much of my instincts didn't enter into our relationship. They remained dormant, happily dormant. But my days and my nights were so full of this man, I was so dependent on him for so much of the twenty-four hours, that it would have been almost inhuman not to have fallen into some sort of love with him. I kept on telling myself that he was humourless, impersonal, un-funloving, wooden and, finally, most excessively German, but that didn't alter the fact that I listened for his step on the stairs, worshipped the warmth and authority of his body, and was happy at all times to cook and mend and work for him. I admitted to myself that I was becoming a vegetable, a docile *Hausfrau*, walking, in my mind, six paces behind him on the street like some native bearer, but I also had to admit that I was happy, contented and carefree, and that I didn't really yearn for any other kind of life. There were moments when I wanted to break out of the douce, ordered cycle of the days, shout and sing and generally create hell, but I told myself that these impulses were basically anti-social, unfeminine, chaotic and psychologically unbalanced. Kurt had made me understand these things. For him, symmetry, the even tempo, the right thing in the right place, the calm voice, the measured opinion, love on Wednesdays and Saturdays (after a light dinner!) were the way to happiness and away from what he described as 'The Anarchic Syndrome'—i.e., smoking and drinking, phenobarbital, jazz, promiscuous sleeping-about, fast cars, slimming, Negroes and their new republics, homosexuality, the abolition of the death penalty and a host of other deviations from what he described as *Naturmenschlichkeit*, or, in more words but shorter ones, a way of life more like the ants and the bees. Well, that was all right with me. I had been brought up to the simple life and I was very happy to be back in it after my brief taste of the rackety round of Chelsea pubs and gimcrack journalism, not to mention my drama-fraught affair with Derek, and I did quietly fall into some sort of love with Kurt.

And then, inevitably, it happened.

Soon after we started making regular love, Kurt had steered

me towards a reliable woman doctor who gave me a homely lecture about contraception and fixed me up. But she warned that even these precautions could go wrong. And they did. At first, hoping for the best, I said nothing to Kurt, but then, from many motives—not wanting to carry the secret alone, the faint hope that he might be pleased and ask me to marry him, and a genuine fear about my condition—I told him. I had no idea what his reaction might be, but of course I expected tenderness, sympathy, and at least a show of love. We were standing by the door of my bedroom, preparatory to saying goodnight. I hadn't a stitch of clothes on, while he was fully dressed. When I had finished telling him, he quietly disengaged my arms from round his neck, looked my body up and down with what I can only call a mixture of anger and contempt, and reached for the door handle. Then he looked me coldly in the eyes, said very softly, 'So?' and walked out of the room and shut the door quietly behind him.

I went and sat down on the edge of my bed and stared at the wall. What had I done? What had I said wrong? What did Kurt's behaviour mean? Then, weak with foreboding, I got into bed and cried myself to sleep.

I was right to cry. The next morning, when I called for him downstairs for our usual walk to the office, he had already gone out. When I got to the office, the communicating door with mine was closed, and when, after a quarter of an hour or so, he opened the door and said we must have a talk, his face was icily cold. I went into his office and sat down with the desk between us: an employee being interviewed by the boss—being sacked, as it turned out.

The burden of his speech, delivered in matter-of-fact, impersonal tones, was this. In a comradely liaison such as we had enjoyed, and it had indeed been most enjoyable, it was essential that matters should run smoothly, in an orderly fashion. We had been (yes, 'had been') good friends, but I would agree that there had never been any talk of marriage, of anything more permanent than a satisfactory understanding between comrades (that word again!). It had indeed been a most pleasant relationship, but now, through the fault of one of the partners (me alone, I suppose!), this had happened, and now a radical solution must be found for a problem that contained elements of embarrassment and even of danger for our life-paths. Marriage—alas, for he had an excellent opinion of my qualities and above all of my physical beauty—was out of the question. Apart from other considerations, he had inherited strong views about mixed blood (Heil Hitler!) and when he married, it would be into the Teutonic strain. Accordingly, and with sincere regret, he had come to certain decisions. The most important was that I must have an immediate operation. Three months was already a dangerous delay. This would be a simple matter. I would fly to Zürich and stay at one of the hotels near the Hauptbahnhof. Any taxi driver would take me there from the airport. I would ask the concierge for the name of the hotel doctor—there were excellent doctors in Zürich—and I would consult him. He would understand the situation. All Swiss doctors did. He would suggest that my blood pressure was too high or too low, or that my nerves were not in a fit state to support the strain of childbirth. He would speak to a gynaecologist—there were superb gynaecologists in Zürich—and I would visit this man who would confirm what the doctor had said and sign a paper to that effect. The gynaecologist would make a reservation at a clinic and the whole matter would be solved inside a week. There would be complete discretion. The procedure was perfectly legal in Switzerland, and I would not even have to show my passport. I could give any name I chose—a married name, naturally. The cost would however be high. Perhaps as much as one hundred, or even one hundred and fifty pounds. That also he had seen to. He reached into the drawer of his desk, took out an envelope and slid it across the table. It would be reasonable, after nearly two years' excellent service, for me to receive one month's salary in lieu of notice. That was one hundred and twenty pounds. Out of his own pocket he had taken the liberty of adding fifty pounds to cover the air fare, tourist class, and leave something over for emergencies. The whole sum was in Reichsmarks to avoid any problem over the exchange.

Kurt smiled tentatively, waiting for my thanks and congratulations for his efficiency and generosity. He must have been put out by the expression of blank horror on my face, because he hurried on. Above all, I must not worry. These unfortunate things happened in life. They were painful and untidy. He himself was most distressed that so happy a relationship, one of the happiest in his experience, should come to an end. As alas it had to. He added finally that he hoped I understood.

I nodded and got to my feet. I picked up the envelope, took one last look at the golden hair, the mouth I had loved, the strong shoulders, and feeling the tears coming, I walked quickly out of the room and shut the door softly behind me.

Before I met Kurt, I had been a bird with a wing down. Now I had been shot in the other.

6 / *GO WEST, YOUNG WOMAN*

At the end of August, when all this happened, Zürich was as gay as this sullen city can be. The clear, glacier water of the lake was bright with sailing-boats and water skiers, the public beaches were thronged with golden bathers and the glum Bahnhofplatz, and the Bahnhofstrasse that is the pride of the town, clattered with rucksacked Jugend who had business with the mountains. The healthy, well-ordered carnival atmosphere rasped on my raw nerves and filled my sick heart with mixed anguish. This was the Kurt's-eye view of life—*Naturfreude*, the simple existence of simple animals. He and I had shared such a life and on the surface it had been good. But blond hair and clear eyes and sunburn are no thicker than the paint on a woman's face. They are just another kind of gloss. A trite reflection, of course, but I had now been let down both by the worldliness of Derek and by the homespun of Kurt and I was prepared to lose confidence in every man. It wasn't that I had expected Kurt to marry me, or Derek. I had just expected them to be kind and to behave like that idiotic word 'gentlemen'—to be gentle with me, as I, I thought, had been gentle with them. That, of course, had been the trouble. I had been too gentle, too accommodating. I had had the desire to please (and to take pleasure, but that had been secondary), and that had marked me as easy meat, expendable. Well, that was the end of that! From now on I would take and not give. The world had shown me its teeth. I would show mine. I had been wet behind the ears. Now I was dry. I stuck my chin out like a good little Canadian (well, a fairly good little Canadian!), and having learnt to take it, decided for a change to dish it out.

The business of my abortion, not to mince words, was good training for my new role. The concierge at my hotel looked at me with the world-weary eyes of all concierges and said that the hotel doctor was on holiday but that there was another who was equally proficient. (Did he know? Did he guess?) Dr Süsskind examined me and asked if I had enough money. When I said I had, he seemed disappointed. The gynaecologist was more explicit. It seemed that he had a chalet. Hotels in Zürich were so expensive. Would I not care to have a period of rest before the operation? I looked at him with stony eyes and said that the British Consul, who was my uncle, had invited me to recuperate with his family and I would be glad if I could enter the clinic without any delay. It was he who had recommended Dr Süsskind. No doubt Herr Doktor Braunschweig knew the Consul?

My hocus-pocus was just good enough. It had been delivered with my new decisive manner and the gambit had been thought out beforehand. The bifocals registered shock. There were coolly fervent explanations and a hasty telephone call to the clinic. Yes, indeed. Tomorrow afternoon. Just with my overnight things.

It was as mentally distressing but as physically painless as I had expected, and three days later I was back in my hotel. My mind was made up. I flew back to England, stayed at the new circular Ariel Hotel near London Airport until I had got rid of my few small belongings and paid my bills, and then I made an appointment with the nearest Vespa dealer, in Hammersmith, and went to see him.

My plan was to go off on my own, for at least a year, and see the other half of the world. I had had London. Life there had hit me with a hard left and right, and I was groggy on my feet. I decided that I just didn't belong to the place. I didn't understand Derek's sophisticated world, and I didn't know how to manage the clinical, cold-eyed, modern 'love' that Kurt had offered me. I told myself that it was because I had too much 'heart'. Neither of these men had wanted my heart, they had just wanted my body. The fact that I fell back on this age-old moan of the discarded woman to explain my failure to hold either of these men, was, I later decided, a more important clue to my failure than this business of 'heart'. The truth of the matter was that I was just too simple to survive in the big-town jungle. I was easy prey for the predators. I was altogether too 'Canadian' to compete with Europe. So be it! I was simple, so I would go back to the simple lands. But not to sit and mope and vegetate. I would go there to explore, to adventure. I would follow the Fall right down through America, working my way as waitress, baby-sitter, receptionist, until I got to Florida, and there I would get a job on a newspaper and sit in the sunshine until the Spring. And then I would think again.

Once I had made up my mind, the details of my plan absorbed me, driving out my misery, or at least keeping it at bay, and anaesthetizing my sense of sin and shame and failure. I went to the American Automobile Association in Pall Mall, joined it and got the maps I needed, and talked to them about transport. The prices of second-hand cars in America were too high, as were the running costs, and I suddenly fell in love with the idea of a motor scooter. At first it seemed ridiculous, the idea of taking on the great transcontinental highways with such a tiny machine, but the thought of being out in the open air, doing around a hundred miles to the gallon, not having to worry about garages, travelling light and, let's admit it, being something of a sensation wherever I went, made up my mind, and the Hammersmith dealer did the rest.

I knew something about machinery—every North American child is brought up with motor-cars—and I weighed up the attractions of the little 125-cc model and of the sturdier, faster 150-cc Gran Sport. Of course, I plumped for the sporty one with its marvellous acceleration and a top speed of nearly sixty. It would only do around eighty miles to the gallon, compared with the smaller one's hundred, but I told myself that gas was cheap in America and that I must have the speed or I would take months to get south. The dealer was enthusiastic. He pointed out that in bad weather, or if I got tired, I could just put the thing on a train for a stretch. He could get about thirty pounds purchase tax off the price of one hundred and ninety pounds by delivering it to a ship that would get it over to Canada in ten days. That would give me extra money to spend on spares and de luxe accessories. I didn't need any pressurizing. We did one or two runs up and down the by-pass, with the dealer sitting on the back, and the Vespa went like a bird and was as easy to drive as a bicycle. So I signed up for it, bought a leopard-skin cover for the seat and spare-wheel, racy-looking de luxe wheel-trims, a rear mirror, a luggage rack, white saddle-bags that went beautifully with the silver finish of the body, a Perspex sports windscreen and a white crash helmet that made me feel like Pat Moss. The dealer gave me some good ideas about clothes, and I went to a store and bought white overalls with plenty of zips, some big goggles with soft fur round the edges and a rather dashing pair of lined black kid motor-cycling gloves. After this I sat down in my hotel with the maps and planned my route for the first stage down from Quebec. Then I booked myself on the cheapest Trans-Canada flight to Montreal, cabled Aunt Florence, and, on a beautiful first-of-September morning, I was off.

It was strange and lovely to be back after nearly six years. My aunt said she could hardly recognize me, and I was certainly surprised by Quebec. When I had left it, the fortress had seemed vast and majestic. Now it seemed like a large toy edifice out of Disneyland. Where it had been awesome, I found, irreverently, that it looked made out of papier-mâché. And the giant battles between the Faiths, in which I had once thought myself to be on the point of being crushed, and the deep schisms between the Canadiennes and the rest, were now reduced, with my new perspective, to parish-pump squabbling. Half ashamed, I found myself contemptuous of the screaming provincialism of the town, of the dowdy peasants who lived in it, and of the all-pervading fog of snobbery and petit bourgeoisie. No wonder, a child of all this, that I had been ill-equipped for the great world outside! The marvel was that I had survived at all.

I was careful to keep these thoughts from my aunt, though I suspect that she was just as startled and perhaps shocked by the gloss that my 'finishing' in Europe had achieved. She must have found me very much the town mouse, however gangling and simple I might feel inside, and she plied me with questions to discover how deep the gloss went, how much I had been sullied by the fast life I must have led. She would have fainted at the truth, and I was careful to say that, while there had been flirtations, I had returned unharmed and heart-whole from the scarlet cities across the water. No, there had not even been a temporary engagement. No lord, not even a commoner, I could truthfully say, had proposed to me, and I had left no boy-friend behind. I don't think she believed this. She was complimentary about my looks. I had become *'une belle fille'*. It seemed that I had developed *'beaucoup de tempérament'*—a French euphemism for 'sex appeal'—or at any rate the appearance of it, and it seemed incredible to her that at twenty-three there was no man in my life. She was horrified at my plans, and painted a doomful picture of the dangers that awaited me on the road. America was full of gangsters. I would be knocked down on the highway and *'ravagé'*. Anyway, it was unladylike to travel on a scooter. She hoped that I would be careful to ride side-saddle. I explained that my Vespa was a most respectable machine and, when I went to Montreal and, thrilling with every mile, rode it back to the house, in my full regalia, she was slightly mollified, while commenting dubiously that I would *'faire sensation'*.

And then, on September 15th, I drew a thousand dollars in American Express travellers' cheques from my small bank balance, scientifically packed my saddle-bags with what I thought would be a minimum wardrobe, kissed Aunt Florence goodbye and set off down the St Lawrence on Route 2.

Route 2 from Quebec southwards to Montreal could be one of the most beautiful roads in the world if it weren't for the clutter of villas and bathing huts that have mushroomed along it since the war. It follows the great river exactly, clinging to the north bank, and I knew it well from bathing picnics as a child. But the St Lawrence Seaway had been opened since then, and the steady stream of big ships with their thudding engines and haunting sirens and whistles were a new thrill.

The Vespa hummed happily along at about forty. I had decided to stick to an average daily run of between a hundred and fifty and two hundred miles, or about six hours' actual driving, but I had no intention of being bound by any schedule. I wanted to see everything. If there was an intriguing side road, I would go up it, and, if I came to a beautiful or interesting place, I would stop and look at it.

A good invention in Canada and the northern part of the States is the 'picnic area'—clearings carved out of the forest or beside a lake or river with plenty of isolated rough-hewn benches and tables tucked away among the trees for privacy. I proposed to use these for luncheon every day when it wasn't raining, not buying expensive foods at stores, but making egg-and-bacon sandwiches in toast before I left each night's motel. They, with fruit and a Thermos of coffee, would be my mid-day meal and I would make up each evening with a good dinner. I budgeted for a daily expenditure of fifteen dollars. Most motels cost eight dollars single, but there are state taxes added, so I made it nine plus coffee and a roll for breakfast. Gas would not be more than a dollar a day and that left five for luncheon and dinner, an occasional drink and the few cigarettes I smoked. I wanted to try and keep inside this. The Esso map and route I had, and the AAA literature, listed countless sights to see after I had crossed the border—I would be going right through the Red Indian country of Fenimore Cooper, and then across some of the great battlefields of the American Revolution, for instance—and many of them cost around a dollar entrance fee. But I thought I would get by, and if on some days I didn't, I would eat less on others.

The Vespa was far more stable than I had expected, and wonderfully easy to run. As I got better at the twist-grip gears, I began really to drive the little machine instead of just riding on it. The acceleration—up to fifty in twenty seconds—was good enough to give the ordinary American sedan quite a shock, and I soared up hills like a bird with the exhaust purring sweetly under my tail. Of course I had to put up with a good deal of wolf-whistling from the young, and grinning and hand-waving from the old, but I'm afraid I rather enjoyed being something of the sensation my aunt had predicted and I smiled with varying sweetness at all and sundry. The shoulders of most North American roads are bad and I had been afraid that people would crowd my tiny machine and that I would be in constant trouble with potholes, but I suppose I looked such a fragile little outfit that other drivers gave me a wide berth and I usually had the whole of the inside lane of the highway to myself.

Things went so well that first day that I managed to get through Montreal before nightfall and twenty miles on down Route 9 that would take me over the border into New York State the next morning. I put up at a place called The Southern Trail Motel, where I was treated as if I was Amelia Earhart or Amy Mollison—a rather pleasurable routine that I became accustomed to—and, after a square meal in the cafeteria and the shy acceptance of one drink with the proprietor, I retired to bed feeling excited and happy. It had been a long and wonderful day. The Vespa was a dream, and my whole plan was working out fine.

I had taken one day to do the first two hundred miles. I took nearly two weeks to cover the next two hundred and fifty. There was no mystery about it. Once over the American border, I began to wander around the Adirondacks as if I was on a late summer holiday. I won't go into details since this is not a travelogue, but there was hardly an old fort, museum, waterfall, cave or high mountain I didn't visit—not to mention the dreadful 'Storylands', 'Adventure Towns' and mock 'Indian Reservations' that got my dollar. I just went on a kind of sightseeing splurge that was part genuine curiosity but mostly wanting to put off the day when I would have to leave these lakes and rivers and forests and hurry on south to the harsh Eldollarado of the super-highways, the hot-dog stands and the ribboning lights of neon.

It was at the end of these two weeks that I found myself at Lake George, the dreadful hub of tourism in the Adirondacks that has somehow managed to turn the history and the forests and the wildlife into honkytonk. Apart from the rather imposing stockade fort and the harmless steamers that ply up to

Fort Ticonderoga and back, the rest is a gimcrack nightmare of concrete gnomes, Bambi deer and toadstools, shoddy food-stalls selling 'Big Chief Hamburgers' and 'Minnehaha Candy Floss', and 'Attractions' such as 'Animal Land' ('Visitors may hold and photograph costumed chimps'), 'Gaslight Village' ('Genuine 1890 gas-lighting'), and 'Storytown USA', a terrifying babyland nightmare which I need not describe. It was here that I fled away from the horrible mainstream that Route 9 had become, and took to the dusty side road through the forest that was to lead me to the Dreamy Pines Motor Court and to the armchair where I have been sitting remembering just exactly how I happened to get here.

Part Two / ***Them***

7 / 'COME INTO MY PARLOUR . . .'

The rain was hammering down just as hard, its steady roar providing a background to the gurgling torrents from the downspouts at the four corners of the building. I looked forward to bed. How soundly I would sleep between the sheets in the spotless little cabin—those percale sheets that featured in the advertisements for the motel! How luxurious the Elliott Frey beds, Magee custom-designed carpets, Philco television and air-conditioning, Icemagic ice-makers, Acrilan blankets and Simmons Vivant furniture ('Our phenolic laminate tops and drawers are immune to cigarette burns, alcohol stains')—in fact all those refinements of modern motel luxury down to Acrylite shower enclosures, Olsonite Pearlescent lavatory seats and Delsey 'bathroom tissue', otherwise lavatory paper ('in modern colours to harmonize with contemporary décor') that would be mine, and mine alone, tonight!

Despite all these gracious trimmings, plus a beautiful site, it seemed that The Dreamy Pines was in a bad way, and, when I had come upon it two weeks before, there were only two overnighters in the whole place and not a single reservation for the last fortnight of the season.

Mrs Phancey, an iron-grey woman with bitter, mistrustful eyes and a grim slit of a mouth, was at the desk when I came in that evening. She had looked sharply at me, a lone girl, and at my meagre saddle-bags, and, when I pushed the Vespa over to Number 9, she followed me with my card in her hand to check that I had not entered a false vehicle licence. Her husband, Jed, was more genial, but I soon understood why when the back of his hand brushed against my breast as, later in the cafeteria, he put the coffee in front of me. Apparently he doubled as handyman and short-order cook and, while his pale brown eyes moved over me like slugs, he complained whiningly about how much there was to do around the place getting it ready for closing date and constantly being called away from some job to fry eggs for parties of transients. It seemed they were the managers for the owner. He lived in Troy. A Mr Sanguinetti. 'Big shot. Owns plenty property down on Cohoes Road. Riverfront property. And The Trojan Horse—roadhouse on Route 9, outside Albany. Maybe you know the joint?' When I said I didn't, Mr Phancey looked sly. 'You ever want some fun, you go along to The Horse. Better not go alone, though. Pretty gal like you could get herself roughed up. After the 15th, when I get away from here, you could give me a call. Phancey's the name. In the phone book. Be glad to escort you, show you a good time.' I thanked him, but said I was just passing through the district on my way south. Could I have a couple of fried eggs, sunnyside up, and bacon?

But Mr Phancey wouldn't leave me alone. While I ate, he came and sat at my little table and told me some of his dull life-story and, in between episodes, slipped in questions about me and my plans—what parents I had, didn't I mind being so far from home, did I have any friends in the States, and so on—innocuous questions, put, it seemed to me, with normal curiosity. He was after all around forty-five, old enough to be my father, and though he was obviously a dirty old man, they were a common enough breed, and anyway Mrs Phancey was keeping an eye on us from the desk at the other end of the room.

Mr Phancey finally left me and went over to his wife and, while I smoked a cigarette and finished my second cup of coffee ('No charge, miss. Compliments of The Dreamy Pines'), I heard them talking in a low voice over something that, because of an occasional chuckle, seemed to give them satisfaction. Finally Mrs Phancey came over, clucking in a motherly fashion about my adventurous plans ('My, oh, my! What will you modern girls be doing next?'), and then she sat down and, looking as winsome as she knew how, said why didn't I stop over for a few days and have a rest and earn myself a handful of dollars into the bargain? It seemed their receptionist had walked out twenty-four hours before and, what with the housekeeping and tidying-up before they closed the place for the season, they would have no time to man the desk. Would I care to take on the job of receptionist for the final two weeks—full board and thirty dollars a week?

Now it happened that I could do very well with those sixty dollars and some free food and lodging. I had overspent at least fifty dollars on my tourist spree, and this would just about square my books. I didn't much care for the Phanceys, but I told myself that they were no worse than the sort of people I had expected to meet on my travels. Besides, this was the first job I had been offered and I was rather curious to see how I would make out. Perhaps, too, they would give me a reference at the end of my time and this might help with other motel jobs on my way south. So, after a bit of polite probing, I said the idea would be fine. The Phanceys seemed very pleased and Millicent, as she had now become, showed me the registration system, told me to watch out for people with little luggage and big station-wagons, and took me on a quick tour of the establishment.

The business about the station-wagons opened my eyes to the seamy side of the motel business. It seemed that there were people, particularly young couples just married and in process of setting up house, who would check in at some lonely motel carrying at least the minimum 'passport' of a single suitcase. This suitcase would in fact contain nothing but a full set of precision tools, together with false licence plates for their roomy station-wagon that would be parked in the car-port alongside their cabin door. After locking themselves in and waiting for the lights to go out in the office, the couple would set to work on inconspicuous things like loosening the screws of the bathroom fixtures, testing the anchoring of the TV set and so on. Once the management had gone to bed, they would really get down to it, making neat piles of bedding, towels and shower curtains, dismantling light-fixtures, bed-frames, lavatory-seats and even the lavatories themselves if they had plumbing knowledge. They worked in darkness of course, with pencil torches, and, when everything was ready, say around two in the morning, they would quietly carry everything through the door into the car-port and pile it into the station-wagon. The last job would be to roll up the carpets and use them, the reverse side up, as tarpaulins to cover the contents of the station-wagon. Then change the plates and softly away with their new bedroom suite all ready to lay out in their unfurnished flat many miles away in another State!

Two or three hauls like that would also look after the living-room and spare bedroom and they would be set up for life. If they had a garden, or a front porch, a few midnight forays around the rich, out-of-town 'swimming-pool' residences would take care of the outdoor furniture, children's heavy playthings, perhaps even the lawn-mower and sprinklers.

Mrs Phancey said the motels had no defence against this sort of attack. Everything was screwed down that could be screwed down, and marked with the name of the motel. The only hope was to smell the marauders when they registered and then either turn them away or sit up all night with a shotgun. In cities, motels had other problems—prostitutes who set up shop, murderers who left corpses in the shower, and occasional holdups for the money in the cash register. But I was not to worry. Just call for Jed if I smelled trouble. He could act real tough and he had a gun. And, with this cold comfort, I was left to ponder on the darker side of the motel industry.

Of course it all turned out perfectly all right and the job was no problem. In fact there was so little to do that I did rather wonder why the Phanceys had bothered to take me on. But they were lazy and it wasn't their money they were paying me and I guessed that part of the reason was that Jed thought he had found himself an easy lay. But that also was no problem. I just had to dodge his hands and snub him icily on an average of once a day and hook a chair under my door handle when I went to bed to defeat the pass-key he tried on my second night.

We had a few overnighters in the first week and I found that I was expected to lend a hand with the housekeeping, but that too was all right with me, and anyway the customers slacked off, until, after October 10th, there wasn't a single one.

Apparently October 15th is a kind of magical date in this particular holiday world. Everything closes down on that day, except along the major highways.

It is supposed to be the beginning of winter. There is the hunting season coming up, but the rich hunters have their own hunting clubs and camps in the mountains, and the poor ones take their cars to one or another of the picnic areas and climb up into the forests before dawn to get their deer. Anyway, around October 15th the tourists disappear from the scene and there is no more easy money to be made in the Adirondacks.

As closing day came nearer, there was a good deal of talk on the telephone between the Phanceys and Mr Sanguinetti in Troy, and on the 11th Mrs Phancey told me casually that she and Jed would be leaving for Troy on the 13th and would I mind staying in charge that night and handing over the keys to Mr Sanguinetti, who would be coming up finally to close the place around noon on the 14th?

It seemed a vague sort of arrangement to leave an unknown girl in charge of such a valuable property, but it was explained that the Phanceys would be taking the cash and the register and the stock of food and drinks with them, and all I had to do was switch off the lights and lock up before I went to bed. Mr Sanguinetti would be coming up with trucks for the rest of the movables the next morning. Then I could be on my way. So I said yes, that would be all right, and Mrs Phancey beamed and said I was a very good girl, but when I asked if she would give me a reference, she got cagey and said she would have to leave that to Mr Sanguinetti, but she would make a point of telling him how helpful I had been.

So the last day was spent packing things into their station-wagon until the stores and cafeteria were empty of everything except plenty of bacon and eggs and coffee and bread for me and for the truckers to eat when they came up.

That last day I had expected the Phanceys to be rather nice to me. After all we had got on all right together and I had gone out of my way to be helpful about everything. But oddly enough, they were just the reverse. Mrs Phancey ordered me about as if I was a skivvy, and Jed became tough and nasty in his leching, using filthy words even when his wife was in earshot and quite openly reaching for my body whenever he got within range. I couldn't understand the change. It was as if they had had what they wanted out of me and could now discard me with contempt—and even, it seemed to me, almost with loathing. I got so furious that I finally went to Mrs

Phancey and said I was going and could I have my money? But she just laughed, and said. Oh, no. Mr Sanguinetti would be giving me that. They couldn't take a chance of the cutlery being short when he came to count it. After this, and rather than face them at supper, I made myself some jam sandwiches and went and locked myself in my cabin and prayed for the morning, when they would be gone. And, as I have said, six o'clock did at last come and I saw the last of the monsters.

And now this was my last night at The Dreamy Pines and tomorrow I would be off again. It had been a slice of life, not totally unpleasant in spite of the Phanceys, and I had learned the fringes of a job that might stand me in good stead. I looked at my watch. It was nine o'clock and here was the doomful WOKO from Albany with its storm bulletin. The Adirondacks would be clear by midnight. So, with any luck, I would have dry roads in the morning. I went behind the cafeteria bar, turned on the electric cooker, and put out three eggs and six slices of hickory-smoked bacon. I was hungry.

And then came a loud hammering on the door.

8 / *DYNAMITE FROM NIGHTMARE-LAND*

My heart went to my mouth. Who could it possibly be? And then I remembered. The Vacancy sign! I had pulled the switch when the lightning struck and I had forgotten to turn the damned thing off. What an idiot! The banging started up again. Well, I would just have to face it, apologize, and send the people on to Lake George. I went nervously across to the door, unlocked it, and held it on the chain.

There was no porch. The neon Vacancy sign made a red halo in the sheet of rain and glittered redly on the shiny black oilskins and hoods of the two men. Behind them was a black sedan. The leading man said politely, 'Miss Michel?'

'Yes, that's me. But I'm afraid the Vacancy sign's on by mistake. The motel's closed down.'

'Sure, sure. We're from Mr Sanguinetti. From his insurance company. Come to make a quick inventory before things get taken away tomorrow. Can we come in out of the rain, miss? Show you our credentials inside. Sure is a terrible night.'

I looked doubtfully from one to the other, but I could see little of the faces under the oilskin hoods. It sounded all right, but I didn't like it. I said nervously, 'But the Phanceys, the managers, they didn't say anything about you coming.'

'Well they should of, miss. I'll havta report that back to Mr

Sanguinetti.' He turned to the man behind him. 'That right, Mister Jones?'

The other man stifled a giggle. Why did he giggle? 'Sure, that's right, Mister Thomson.' He giggled again.

'Okay then, miss. Can we come inside, please? It sure is wetter'n hell out here.'

'Well, I don't know. I was told not to let anyone in. But as it's from Mr Sanguinetti . . .' I nervously undid the chain and opened the door.

They pushed in, shouldering roughly past me, and stood side by side looking the big room over. The man who had been addressed as 'Mr Thomson' sniffed. Black eyes looked at me out of a cold, grey face. 'You smoke?'

'Yes, a little. Why?'

'Reckoned you could have company.' He took the door handle from me, slammed the door, locked it, and put up the chain. The two men stripped off their dripping oilskins and threw them messily down on the floor and, now that I could see them both, I felt in extreme danger.

'Mr Thomson', obviously the leader, was tall and thin, almost skeletal, and his skin had this grey, drowned look as if he always lived indoors. The black eyes were slow-moving, incurious, and the lips thin and purplish like an unstitched wound. When he spoke there was a glint of grey silvery metal from his front teeth and I supposed they had been cheaply capped with steel, as I had heard was done in Russia and Japan. The ears lay very flat and close to the bony, rather box-shaped head and the stiff, greyish-black hair was cut so close to the skull that the skin showed whitely through it. He was wearing a black, sharp-looking single-breasted coat with shoulders padded square, stovepipe trousers so narrow that the bones of his knees bulged through the material, and a grey shirt buttoned up to the throat with no tie. His shoes were pointed in the Italian style and of grey suede. They and the clothes looked new. He was a frightening lizard of a man, and my skin crawled with fear of him.

Where this man was deadly, the other was merely unpleasant—a short, moon-faced youth with wet, very pale blue eyes and fat wet lips. His skin was very white and he had that hideous disease of no hair—no eyebrows and no eyelashes, and none on a head that was as polished as a billiard ball. I would have felt sorry for him if I hadn't been so frightened, particularly as he seemed to have a bad cold and began blowing his nose as soon as he got his oilskins off. Under them he wore a black leather windcheater, grubby trousers and those Mexican saddle-leather boots with straps that they wear in Texas. He looked a young monster, the sort that pulls wings off flies, and I desperately wished that I had dressed in clothes that didn't make me seem so terribly naked.

Sure enough, he now finished blowing his nose and seemed to take me in for the first time. He looked me over, grinning delightedly. Then he walked all round me and came back and gave a long, low whistle. 'Say, Horror,' he winked at the other man. 'This is some bimbo! Git an eyeful of those knockers! And a rear-end to match! Geez, what a dish!'

'Not now, Sluggsy. Later. Git goin' and look those cabins over. Meantime, the lady's goin' to fix us some chow. How you want your eggs?'

The man called Sluggsy grinned at me. 'Scramble 'em, baby. And nice and wet. Like mother makes. Otherwise poppa spank. Right across that sweet little biscuit of yours. Oh boy, oh boy!' He did some little dancing, boxing steps towards me and I backed away to the door. I pretended to be even more frightened than I was, and when he got within range I slapped him as hard as I could across the face and, before he could re-cover from his surprise, I had darted sideways behind a table and picked up one of the little metal chairs and held it with the feet pointing at him.

The thin man gave a short, barking laugh. 'Ixnay, Sluggsy. I said later. Leave the stupid slot be. There's all night for that. Git goin' like I said.'

The eyes in the pale moon-face were now red with excitement. The man rubbed his cheek. The wet lips parted in a slow smile. 'You know what, baby? You just earned yourself one whale of a night. An' it's goin' to be long and slow an' again and again. Get me?'

I looked at them both from behind the raised chair. Inside I was whimpering. These men were dynamite from Nightmareland. Somehow I kept my voice steady. 'Who are you? What's this all about? Let's see those credentials. The next car that comes by, I'll break a window and get help. I'm from Canada. You do anything to me and you'll be in bad trouble tomorrow.'

Sluggsy laughed. 'Tomorrow's tomorrow. What you got to worry about's tonight, baby.' He turned to the thin man. 'Mebbe you better wise her up, Horror. Then mebbe we'll get some co-operation.'

Horror looked across at me. His expression was cold, uninterested. 'Ya shouldn't of hit Sluggsy, lady. The boy's tough. He don't like the dames not to go for him. Thinks it may be on account of his kisser. Been like that since he done a spell in solitary at San Q. Nervous sickness. What's that the docs call it, Sluggsy?'

Sluggsy looked proud. He brought the Latin words out carefully. '*Alopecia totalis.* That means no hair, see? Not a one.' He gestured at his body. 'Not here, or here, or here. What d'ya know about that, eh, bimbo?'

Horror continued. 'So Sluggsy gets mad easy. Thinks he ain't had a fair deal from society. You had that puss of his, mebbe you'd be the same. So he's what we call in Troy an enforcer. Guys hire him to make other guys do what they want, if you get me. He's on Mr Sanguinetti's roll, and Mr Sanguinetti thought he and I better come along and keep an eye on this joint till the truckers come. Mr Sanguinetti didn't care for a young lady like you bein' all alone here at night. So he sent us along for company. Ain't that so, Sluggsy?'

'That's the spiel. Sure is,' he giggled. 'Just to keep you company, bimbo. Keep the wolves away. With them statistics of yours, there must be times when you need protection real bad. Right?'

I lowered the chair on to the table top. 'Well, what are your names? What about these credentials?'

There was a single tin of Maxwell House coffee on the shelf above the bar counter, all by itself. Sluggsy suddenly swivelled and his right hand—I hadn't even seen him draw a gun—shot flame. There was the crash of gunfire. The tin jumped sideways and then fell. In mid-air Sluggsy hit it again and there was a brown explosion of coffee. Then a deafening silence in which the last empty shell tinkled away on the floor. Sluggsy turned back to me. His hands were empty. The gun had gone. His eyes were dreamy with pleasure at his marksmanship. He said softly, 'How's them for credentials, baby?'

The small cloud of blue smoke had reached me, and I smelled the cordite. My legs were trembling. I said, scornfully I hope, 'That's a lot of wasted coffee. Now, what about your names?'

The thin man said, 'The lady's right. You didn't ought to of spilled that java, Sluggsy. But ya see, lady, that's why they call him Sluggsy, on account he's smart with the hardware. Sluggsy Morant. Me, I'm Sol Horowitz. They call me "Horror". Can't say why. Kin you, Sluggsy?'

Sluggsy giggled. 'Mebbe one time you gave some guy a

scare, Horror. Mebbe a whole bunch of guys. Leastwise that's what they tell me.'

Horror made no comment. He said quietly, 'Okay. Let's go! Sluggsy, see to the cabins like I said. Lady, you make us some chow. Keep ya nose clean and co-operate and ya won't get hurt. Okay?'

Sluggsy looked me over greedily. He said, 'Not much, that is. Eh, bimbo?' and walked over to the key rack behind the desk and took down all the keys and let himself out through the back entrance. I put down the chair, and, as coolly as I knew how, but painfully aware of my toreador pants, walked across the room and went behind the counter.

The man called Horror sauntered slowly over to the cafeteria table farthest from me. He pulled a chair away from the table, twisted it in his hand and pushed it between his legs. He sat down and leaned his folded arms along the back and rested his chin on them and watched me with unwavering, indifferent eyes. He said softly, so softly that I could only just hear him, 'I'll take mine scrambled too, lady. Plenty crisp bacon. Buttered toast. Howsabout coffee?'

'I'll see what's left.' I got down on my hands and knees behind the bar. The tin had four holes right through it. There was about an inch of coffee left and a whole lot scattered over the floor. I put the tin aside and scraped what I could from the floor on to a plate, not caring how much dust went with it. The unspoiled remains of the tin I would keep for myself.

I spent about five minutes down there, taking my time, desperately trying to think, to plan. These men were gangsters. They worked for this Mr Sanguinetti. That seemed certain because they had got my name from him or from the Phanceys. The rest of their story was lies. They had been sent up here, through the storm, for a purpose. What was it? They knew I was a Canadian, a foreigner, and that I could easily go to the police the next day and get them into trouble. The man called Sluggsy had been in San Quentin. And the other? Of course! That was why he looked grey and sort of dead! He had probably just come out of prison, too. He smelled of it, somehow. So I could get them into real trouble, tell the police that I was a journalist, that I was going to write up what happened to girls alone in the States. But would I be believed? That Vacancy sign! I was alone in the place, yet I had left it on. Wasn't that because I wanted company? Why had I dressed up like that, to kill, if I had expected to be alone? I dodged away from that line of thought. But, to get back. What did these two men want here? They had an ordinary car. If they had wanted to clean the place out, they would have brought a truck. Perhaps they really had been sent up to guard the place, and they just treated me as they did because that was the way gangsters behaved. But how much worse were they going to get? What was going to happen to me tonight?

I got to my feet and began to busy myself with the cooking. Better give them what they wanted. There must be no excuse for them to set on me.

Jed's apron was rolled up and thrown into a corner. I picked it up and put it round my waist. A weapon? There was an ice-pick in the cutlery drawer and a long, very sharp carving knife. I took the pick and stuck it handle first down the front of my pants under the apron. The knife I hid under a dish-cloth beside the sink. I left the cutlery drawer open and lined up beside it a row of glasses and cups for throwing. Childish? It was all I had.

Every now and then I glanced across the room. Always the thin man's eyes were on me, old in crime and its counter-moves, knowing what was in my mind, what defences I was preparing. I sensed this, but I went on with my little preparations, thinking, as I had at the English school, 'When they hurt me, and I know they're meaning to hurt me, I must somehow hurt them back. When they get me, rape me, kill me, they mustn't find it easy.'

Rape? Kill? What did I think was really going to happen to me? I didn't know. I only knew that I was in desperate trouble. The men's faces said so—the indifferent face and the greedy face. They both had it in for me. Why? I didn't know. But I was absolutely certain of it.

I had broken eight eggs into a bowl and had whipped them gently with a fork. The huge chunk of butter had melted in the saucepan. Beside it, in the frying pan, the bacon was beginning to sizzle. I poured the eggs into the saucepan and began to stir. While my hands concentrated, my mind was busy on ways to escape. Everything depended on whether the man called Sluggsy, when he came back from his inspection, remembered to lock the back door. If he didn't, I could make a dash for it. There would be no question of using the Vespa. I hadn't run it for a week. Priming the carburettor, and the three kicks that might be necessary to start it from cold, would be too long. I would have to leave my belongings, all my precious money, and just go like a hare to right or left, get round the end of the cabins and in among the trees. I reflected that of course I wouldn't run to the right. The lake behind the cabins would narrow my escape route. I would run to the left. There, there was nothing but miles of trees. I would be soaked to the skin within a few yards of the door, and freezing cold for the rest of the night. My feet, in their stupid little sandals, would be cut to ribbons. I might easily get lost into the bargain. But those were problems I would have to cope with. The main thing was to get away from these men. Nothing else mattered.

The eggs were ready and I heaped them out, still very soft, on to a flat dish and added the bacon round the sides. I put the pile of toast from the Toastmaster on another plate, together with a slab of butter still in its paper, and put the whole lot on a tray. I was glad to see that plenty of dust rose to the top when I poured boiling water over the coffee, and I hoped it would choke them. Then I carried the tray out from behind the bar and, feeling more respectable in my apron, took it over to where the thin man was sitting.

As I put it down, I heard the back door open and then slam shut. There had been no click of a lock. I looked quickly round. Sluggsy's hands were empty. My heart began to beat wildly. Sluggsy came over to the table. I was taking things off the tray. He looked the meal over and came swiftly behind me and seized me round the waist, nuzzling his ghastly face into my neck. 'Just like mother made 'em, baby. Howsabout you and me shacking up together? If you can ——— like you can cook, you're the gal of my dreams. What say, bimbo? Is it a deal?'

I had my hand on the coffee pot and he was just going to get the boiling contents slung over my shoulder. Horror saw my intention. He said sharply, 'Leave her be, Sluggsy. I said later.' The words came out like a whiplash, and at once Sluggsy let me go. The thin man said, 'Ya nearly got ya eyeballs fried. Ya want to watch this dame. Quit foolin' around and sit down. We're on a job.'

Sluggsy's face showed bravado, but also obedience. 'Have a heart, pal! I want a piece of this baby. But now!' But he pulled out a chair and sat down, and I moved quickly away.

The big radio and TV was on a pedestal near the back door. It had been playing softly all this time, although I had been quite unconscious of it. I went to the machine and fiddled with the dials, putting the volume up. The two men were talking to each other quietly and there was the clatter of cutlery. Now or never! I measured my distance to the door handle and dived to the left.

9 / *THEN I BEGAN TO SCREAM*

I heard a single bullet crash into the metal frame of the door, and then, with my hand cushioning the ice-pick so it didn't stick into me, I was running hell for leather across the wet grass. Mercifully the rain had let up, but the grass was soaking and slippery under my hopeless flat soles and I knew I wasn't making enough speed. I heard a door crash open behind me and Sluggsy's voice shouted, 'Hold it, or you're cold turkey!' I began to weave, but then the shots came, carefully, evenly spaced, and bees whipped past me and slapped into the grass. Another ten yards and I would be at the corner of the cabins and out of the light. I dodged and zigzagged, my skin quivering as it waited for the bullet. A window in the last cabin tinkled with broken glass and I was round the corner. As I dived into the soaking wood I heard a car start up. What was that for?

It was terrible going. The dripping pines were thick together, their branches overlapping, and they tore at the arms crossed over my face. It was black as pitch and I couldn't see a yard ahead. And then suddenly I could, and I sobbed as I realized what the car was for, for now its blazing headlights were holding me from the edge of the trees. As I tried to dodge the searching eyes, I heard the engine rev to aim the car and immediately they had me again. There was no room for manoeuvre and I just had to make headway in whatever direction the trees allowed me. When would the shooting start up again? I was a bare thirty yards inside the forest. It would be any minute now! My breath was sobbing out of my throat. My clothes had begun to tear and I could feel bruises coming on my feet. I knew I couldn't hold out much longer. I would just have to find the thickest tree and try and lose the lights for a minute and crawl in under the tree and hide. But why no bullets? I stumbled away to the right, found brief darkness, and dived to my knees among the soaking pine needles. There was a tree like any other, its branches sweeping the ground, and I crawled in under them and up against the trunk and waited for the rasping of my breath to quieten down.

And then I heard one of them coming in after me, not softly because that was impossible, but steadily, and stopping every now and then to listen. By now the man, whichever it was, must realize from the silence that I had gone to ground. If he knew anything about tracking, he would soon find where the broken branches and scuffed earth stopped. Then it would only be a question of time. I softly squirmed round to the back of the tree, away from him, and watched the lights from the car hold steady in the glistening wet branches above my head.

The feet and the snapping twigs were coming nearer. Now I could hear the heavy breathing. Sluggsy's voice, very near, said softly, 'Come on out, baby. Or poppa spank real hard. Da game of tag is over. Time to come home to poppa.'

The small eye of a flashlight began searching under the trees, carefully, tree by tree. He knew I was only a few yards away. Then the light stopped and held steady under my tree. Sluggsy said softly, delightedly, 'Coo-ee, baby! Poppa find!'

Had he? I lay still, hardly breathing.

There came the roar and flame of a single shot, and the bullet smacked into the tree-trunk behind my head. 'That's just a hastener, baby. Next time it takes your little footsie off.'

So that was what showed! I said, weary with fright, 'All right. I'll come. But don't shoot!' And I scrambled out on all-fours, thinking hysterically, 'This is a fine way to go to your execution, Viv!'

The man stood there, his pale head fretted with yellow light and black shadows. His gun was pointed at my stomach. He waved it sideways. 'Okay. Get ahead of me. An' if you don't keep moving, you'll get a root in that sweet little keister of yours.'

I stumbled ignominiously through the trees towards the distant, glaring eyes of the car. Hopelessness had me by the throat, and an ache of self-pity. What had I done to deserve this? Why had God picked on me as a victim for these two unknown men? Now they would be really angry. They would hurt me and later almost certainly kill me. But the police would dig the bullets out of me! What evil crime were they engaged on that made them indifferent to the evidence of my dead body? Whatever the crime was, they must be quite confident that there would be no evidence. Because there would be no me! They would bury me, drop me in the lake with a stone round my neck!

I came out through the fringe of the trees. The thin man leant out of the car and called to Sluggsy. 'Okay. Take her back. Don't treat her rough. That's for me.' He put the car into reverse.

Sluggsy came up beside me and his free hand fondled me lasciviously. I just said, 'Don't.' I had no will left to resist.

He said softly, 'You're in trouble, bimbo. Horror's a mean guy. He'll hurt you bad. Now you say "Yes" to me for tonight, and promise to act sweet, and mebbe I can get the heat taken off. Howsabout it, baby?'

I summoned a last ounce of fight. 'I'd rather die than have you touch me.'

'Okay, sweetheart. So you won't give, so I take for myself. I reckon you've earned yourself a rough night. Get me?' He pinched me viciously so that I cried out. Sluggsy laughed delightedly. 'That's right. Sing, baby! Might as well get into practice.'

He pushed me in through the open back door of the lobby block and shut and locked it behind him. The room looked just the same—the lights blazing, the radio hammering out some gay dance tune, everything winking and glittering and polished under the light. I thought of how happy I had been in that room only a few hours before, of the memories I had had in that armchair, some of them sweet, some of them sad. How small now my childish troubles seemed! How ridiculous to talk of broken hearts and lost youth when, just around the corner of my life, these men were coming at me out of the darkness. The cinema in Windsor? It was a small act in a play, almost a farce. Zürich? It was paradise. The true jungle of the world, with its real monsters, only rarely shows itself in the life of a man, a girl, in the street. But it is always there. You take a wrong step, play the wrong card in Fate's game, and you are in it and lost—lost in a world you had never imagined, against which you have no knowledge and no weapons. No compass.

The man called Horror stood in the middle of the room, idle, relaxed, his hands at his sides. He watched me with those incurious eyes. Then he lifted his right hand and crooked a finger. My cold, bruised feet walked towards him. When I was only a few steps away from him I came out of the trance. I suddenly remembered, and my hand came up to the soaking waistband of my pants and I felt the head of the ice-pick under the apron. It was going to be difficult to get it out, to get at the handle. I stopped in front of him. Still holding my eyes, his right hand came up like a snake striking and slapped me, biff-baff, right and left across my face. The tears started from my eyes, but I remembered, and ducked down as if to escape another blow. At the same time, concealed in the movement, I got my right hand down inside the band of my pants, and when I came up I threw myself at him, hitting wildly towards his head. The pick connected, but it was only a glancing blow, and suddenly my arms were gripped from behind and I was pulled back.

Blood was oozing from a cut above the temple of the grey face. As I watched, it trickled down towards the chin. But the face was unmoved. It showed no pain, only a terrifying intensity of purpose, and there was a fleck of red deep inside the black eyes. The thin man stepped up to me. My hand opened and the pick fell to the floor with a clang. It was a reflex action—the child dropping the weapon. I give up! I surrender! Pax!

And then slowly, almost caressingly, he began to hit me, now with his open hand, now with the fist, choosing his targets with refined, erotic cruelty. At first I twisted and bent and kicked, and then I began to scream, while the grey face with the blood-streak and the black holes for eyes watched, and the hands sprang and sprang.

I came to in the shower of my cabin. I was lying naked on the tiles, the tattered, filthy remains of my pretty clothes beside me. Sluggsy, chewing at a wooden toothpick, leaned up against the wall with his hand on the cold tap. His eyes were glistening slits. He turned off the water and I somehow got to my knees. I knew I was going to be sick. I didn't care. I was a tamed, whimpering animal ready to die. I retched.

Sluggsy laughed. He leant over and patted my behind. 'Go

ahead, baby. First thing after a beat-up, everyone vomits. Then clean yourself up nice and put on a nice new outfit and come on over. Those eggs got spoiled with you running off like that. No tricks! Though I guess you ain't got stomach for any more. I'll be watching the cabin from the back door. Now don't take on, baby. No blood. Hardly a bruise. Horror's got a nice touch with the dames. You're sure lucky. He's a hippy guy. If he'd of been real mad, we'd be digging a hole for you right now. Count your blessings, baby. Be seein' ya.'

I heard the door of the cabin bang shut and then my body took over.

It took me half an hour to get myself into some kind of shape, and again and again I just wanted to throw myself on my bed and let the tears go on coming until the men arrived with their guns to finish me off. But the will to live came back into me with the familiar movements of doing my hair and of getting my body, sore and aching and weak with the memory of much greater pain, to do what I wanted, and slowly into the back of my mind there crept the possibility that I might have been through the worst. If not, why was I still alive? For some reason these men wanted me there and not out of the way. Sluggsy was so good with his gun that he could surely have killed me when I made a run for it. His bullets had come close, but hadn't they been just to frighten, to make me stop?

I put on my white overalls. Heaven knew they were impersonal enough, and I put my money into one of the pockets—just in case. Just in case of what? There would be no more escapes. And then, feeling sore and weak as a kitten, I dragged myself over to the lobby.

It was eleven o'clock. The rain was still holding off and a three-quarter moon sailed through fast, scudding clouds, making the forest blink intermittently with white light. Sluggsy was framed in the yellow entrance, leaning against the door, chewing at his toothpick. As I came up, he made way for me. 'That's my baby. Fresh as paint. A little sore here and there, mebbe. Have to sleep on your back later, huh? But that's just what'll suit us, won't it, honey?'

When I didn't answer, he reached out and caught my arm. 'Hey, hey! Where your manners, bimbo? You like some treatment on the other side, mebbe? That also can be arranged.' He made a threatening gesture with his free hand.

'I'm sorry. I didn't mean anything.'

'Okay, okay,' he let me go. 'Now just get on back there and make with the pots and pans. An' don't go getting my gauge up. Or my friend Horror's. Look what you done to that handsome kisser of his.'

The thin man was sitting at his old table. The first-aid box from the reception desk was open in front of him and he had a big square of adhesive across his right temple. I gave him a quick, frightened glance and went behind the serving counter. Sluggsy went over to him and sat down and they began talking together in low voices, occasionally glancing across at me.

Making the eggs and coffee made me feel hungry. I couldn't understand it. Ever since the two men had got in through that door, I had been so tense and frightened I couldn't have swallowed even a cup of coffee. Of course, I was empty from being sick, but in a curious and, I felt, rather shameful way the beating I had been given had in some mysterious fashion relaxed me. The pain, being so much greater than the tension of waiting for it, had unravelled my nerves and there was a curious centre of warmth and peace in my body. I was frightened still, of course—terrified, but in a docile, fatalistic way. At the same time my body said it was hungry, it wanted to get back its strength, it wanted to live.

So I made scrambled eggs and coffee and hot buttered toast for myself as well, and, after I had taken theirs over, I sat down out of sight of them behind the counter and ate mine and then, almost calmly, lit a cigarette. I knew the moment I lit it that it was a foolish thing to do. It called attention to me. Worse, it showed I had recovered, that I was worth baiting again. But the food and the simple business of eating it—of putting salt and pepper on the eggs, sugar into the coffee—had been almost intoxicating. It was part of the old life, a thousand years ago, before the men came. Each mouthful—the forkful of egg, the bit of bacon, the munch of buttery toast—was an exquisite thing that occupied all my senses. Now I knew what it must be like to get some food smuggled into jail, to be a prisoner of war and get a parcel from home, to find water in the desert, to be given a hot drink after being rescued from drowning. The simple act of living, how precious it was! If I got out of this, I would know it for ever. I would be grateful for every breath I breathed, every meal I ate, every night I felt the cool kiss of sheets, the peace of a bed behind a closed, a locked, door. Why had I never known this before? Why had my parents, my lost religion, never taught it to me? Anyway, I knew now. I had found it out for myself. Love of life is born of the awareness of death, of the dread of it. Nothing makes one really grateful for life except the black wings of danger.

These feverish thoughts were born of the intoxication of the food and of eating it alone behind the barricade of the counter. For a few moments I was back in the old life. So, lightheartedly, and to hug the moment to me, I lit the cigarette.

Perhaps a minute later, the mumble of the voices died. Behind 'Tales of the Vienna Woods' coming softly from the radio, I heard a chair being drawn back. Now I felt panic. I put out the cigarette in the dregs of my coffee and got up and began briskly turning taps and clattering the dishes in the metal sink. I didn't look, but I could see Sluggsy coming across the room. He came up to the counter and leaned on it.

I looked up as if surprised. He was still chewing away at a toothpick, flicking it from side to side of his thick-lipped, oval mouth. He had a box of Kleenex that he put on the counter. He wrenched out a handful of tissues and blew his nose and dropped the tissues on the floor. He said in an amiable voice, 'Ya gone an' given me a catarrh, bimbo. All that chasing aroun' in the woods. This trouble of mine, this alopecia thing that kills the hair. You know what that does? That kills the hairs inside the nose too. Together with all the rest. An' you know what that does? That makes your schnozzle dribble bad when you got a cold. You given me a cold, bimbo. That means a box of wipes every twenty-four hours. More, mebbe. Ya ever think of that? Ya ever think of people have no hairs in their snouts? Aargh!' The hairless eyes were suddenly hard with anger. 'You gashes are all the same. Just think of yerselves. To hell with the guys that got troubles! You just go for the good-timers.'

I said quietly, under the noise of the radio, 'I'm sorry for your troubles. Why aren't you sorry for mine?' I spoke quickly, forcefully. 'Why do you two come here and knock me about? What have I done to you? Why don't you let me go? If you do I promise I won't say a word to anyone. I've got a little money. I could give you some of it. Say two hundred dollars. I can't afford any more. I've got to get all the way down to Florida on the rest. Please, won't you let me go?'

Sluggsy let out a hoot of laughter. He turned and called across to the thin man, 'Hey, get out the crying towel, Horror. The slot says she'll hand over two Cs if we let her scram.' The thin man gave a slight shrug of the shoulders, but made no comment. Sluggsy turned back to me. His eyes were hard and without mercy. He said, 'Wise up, bimbo. You're in the act, and you've been given a star part to play. You ought to be tickled to be of so much interest to busy, important guys like Horror and me, and to a big wheel like Mr Sanguinetti.'

'What is the act? What do you want me for?'

Sluggsy said indifferently, 'You'll be wised up come morning. Meanwhiles, howsabout shuttin' that dumb little hashtrap of yours? All this yak is bending my ear. I want some action. That's sweet stuff they're playing. Howsabout you an' me stepping it together? Put on a little show for Horror. Then we'll be off to the hay and make with the bodies. C'mon, chick.' He held out his arms, clicking his fingers to the music and doing some fast steps.

'I'm sorry. I'm tired.'

Sluggsy came back to the counter. He said angrily, 'You've got a big keister giving me that crap. Cheap little hustler! I'll give you something to make you tired.'

Suddenly there was an obscene little black leather cosh in his hand. He brought it down with a dull whack on the counter. It left a deep dent in the formica. He began to move stealthily round the edge of the counter, humming to himself, his eyes holding mine. I backed up into the far corner. This was going to be my last gesture. Somehow I must hurt him back before I went under. My hand felt for the open cutlery drawer and suddenly I dipped in and flung, all in one motion. His duck wasn't quick enough, and the silver spray of knives and forks burst round his head. He put a hand up to his face and backed away, cursing. I hurled some more and then some more, but they only clattered inoffensively round his hunched head. Now the thin man was moving fast across the room. I grabbed the carving knife and made a dash for Sluggsy, but he saw me coming and dodged behind a table. Unhurriedly, Horror took off his coat and wrapped it round his left arm, then they both picked up chairs and, holding the legs out like bulls' horns, they charged me from both sides. I made one ineffectual slash at an arm, and then the knife was knocked out of my hand and all I could do was to get back behind the counter.

Still holding the chair, Sluggsy came in after me and, while I stood facing him, with a plate in each hand, the thin man leant swiftly across the counter and got hold of my hair. I hurled the plates sideways, but they only clattered away across the floor. And then my head was being bent down on to the counter top and Sluggsy was on me.

'Okay, Horror. Let her go. This is for me.'

I felt his powerful arms round me, crushing me, and his face was against mine, kissing me brutally, while his hand went up to the zip at my neck and tore it right down to my waist.

And then came the sharp sound of the buzzer at the front door, and everyone froze.

Part Three / ***Him***

10 / *WHASSAT?*

'Kerist, whassat?' Sluggsy had backed away and his hand was inside his leather jacket.

Horror recovered himself first. There was a cold snarl on his face. 'Git over behind the door, Sluggsy. Hold your fire until I tell you. You,' he spat the words at me, 'get yourself into shape. You've got to front for us. If you don't do it good you're dead. Understand? You'll be shot. Now get over to that door and find out who it is. Tell 'em the same story you told us. Get me? And take that silly expression off your face. No one's going to hurt you if you do what I say. Pull that zip up, dammit!' I was struggling with the thing. It was stuck. 'Well, hold the damn thing together across your chest and get moving. I'll be right behind you. And don't forget, one wrong word and you get blasted through the back. And the guy, too. Now scram over there.'

My heart was beating wildly. Somehow, whatever happened, I was going to save myself!

There was now a loud knocking at the door. I went slowly over, holding the top half of my overalls together. I knew the first thing I had to do!

When I got to the door, Sluggsy leaned sideways and unlocked it. Now everything depended on the speed of my hands. I took hold of the door handle with my left hand and, as I turned it, my right hand let go of the overalls and dived down to the chain and unhooked it. Somebody cursed softly behind me and I felt the prod of a gun in my back, but then I had swung the door wide open, crashing Sluggsy against the wall behind it. I had gambled that, without knowing if it was perhaps the police or a road patrol, they wouldn't shoot. They hadn't. Now all depended on the solitary man who stood on the threshold.

At first glance I inwardly groaned—God, it's another of them! He stood there so quiet and controlled and somehow with the same quality of deadliness as the others. And he wore that uniform that the films make one associate with gangsters—a dark-blue, belted raincoat and a soft black hat pulled rather far down. He was good-looking in a dark, rather cruel way and a scar showed whitely down his left cheek. I quickly put my hand up to hide my nakedness. Then he smiled and suddenly I thought I might be all right.

When he spoke, my heart leaped. He was English! 'I'm sorry. I've got a puncture.' (An American would have said 'a flat'.) 'And I saw the Vacancy sign. Can I have a room for the night?' Now he looked at me with curiosity, seeing that something was wrong.

This was going to be tricky! I might easily get us both killed. I said, 'I'm sorry, but the motel's closed. The Vacancy sign was on by mistake.' While I said this, I crooked the index finger of the hand at my chest, inviting him in. He looked puzzled. I had to give him a lead. 'Is the puncture so bad that you can't get as far as Lake George?'

'Couldn't possibly. I've already come a mile on the rim. The cover'll be gone by now.'

I imperceptibly jerked my head backwards, bidding him to come in. 'Well, the insurance men are here from the owner. I'll have to ask them. You wait there.' Again I beckoned with my finger. Then I turned and took two steps inside, keeping close to the door so that neither of them could bang it shut. But they were standing back, hands in their pockets, looking different kinds of hell at me. The man in the raincoat had taken my hint and he was now well inside. When he saw the two men, his face somehow sharpened, but he said casually, 'I expect you heard all that. Any objection to my spending the night here?'

Sluggsy said contemptuously, 'Kerist! A limey! What is this, the United Nations?'

The thin man said curtly, 'No dice, friend. You heard the lady. The motel's closed. We'll give you a hand changing the wheel and you can be on your way.'

The Englishman said easily, 'It's a bit late at night for that. I'm heading south and I doubt if there's anything on this road this side of Glens Falls. I think I'd prefer to stay here. After all, the Vacancy sign's on.'

'You heard me, mister.' Horror's voice was now tough. He turned to Sluggsy. 'C'mon. We'll give the guy a hand with his flat.' They both took a step towards the door. But the Englishman, bless him, stood his ground.

'It happens that I have friends at Albany, quite important friends. You wouldn't want to lose your motel operator's licence, would you? The sign said "Vacancy", and the place is lit up. I'm tired and I claim a room.' He turned to me. 'Would that give you any trouble?'

I gushed, 'Oh, no! None at all. It won't take me a minute to get a room ready. I'm sure Mr Sanguinetti wouldn't want to do anything to lose his licence?' I turned wide-eyed and innocent towards the two gangsters. They looked as if they were just about to pull their guns, but the thin man moved away and Sluggsy followed him and they talked for a moment in whispers. I took the opportunity to nod urgently and appealingly at the Englishman and he gave me another of those reassuring smiles.

The thin man turned round. 'Okay, limey. You can have the room. But just don't try and lean on us with that Albany guff. Mr Sanguinetti has friends at the capital, too. Mebbe you got a point with that Vacancy sign. But don't push your luck. We're in charge here and what we says goes. Right?'

'That's all right with me. And thanks. I'll get my bag.'

He moved to go out. I said quickly, 'I'll give you a hand.' I hurried ahead of him, tugging furiously at my zip, feeling ashamed of how I must have looked. Blessedly, it suddenly yielded and I pulled it up to my throat.

He came up with me. I said urgently, out of the corner of my mouth—I was sure one of them had come to the door and was watching us—'Thank you! And thank God you came! They were going to murder me. But for God's sake look out. They're gangsters. I don't know what they want. It must be something bad. They shot at me when I tried to escape.'

We came to the car. It was a dark grey two-seater Thunderbird with a soft top in cream, a beautiful thing. I said so. He said shortly that it was hired. He said, 'Come round the other side. Just seem to be admiring the car.' He leaned down and opened the low door and rummaged inside. He said, 'Are they both armed?'

'Yes.'

'How many guns each?'

'Don't know. The small one's a crack shot. At twenty feet or so. Don't know about the other.'

He pulled out a small black suitcase, rested it on the ground and snapped it open. He took something from under the clothes and slipped it into an inside pocket. He fiddled with one side of the case, took some thin black objects out that I took to be cartridge magazines, and stowed them away. Then he snapped the case shut, said, 'Better have plenty of artillery,' banged the door ostentatiously, and stood up. We then both went to the back of the car and knelt down to examine the flat tyre. He said, 'How about the telephone?'

'It's cut off.'

'Give me the cabin next to yours.'

'Of course.'

'All right. Let's go. And keep close to me whatever they do or say.'

'Yes, and thank you.'

He got up and smiled. 'Wait till we're out of this.'

We walked back together. Sluggsy, who had been standing in the doorway, shut the door after us and locked it. As an afterthought, he reached up and switched off the Vacancy sign. He said, 'Here's your key, limey,' and threw it on a table.

I picked it up and looked at the number. Forty, the last one along to the left. I said firmly, 'The gentleman's going to have Number 10, next to mine,' and walked over to the desk, forgetting that Sluggsy had all the other keys.

Sluggsy had followed me. He grinned. 'No dice, baby. We don't know nuthen about this guy. So Horror and me's sleepin' either side of you. Just to see you're not disturbed. Rest of the keys is put away ready for the move. There's just this Number 40 and nuthen else.' He turned to the Englishman. 'Hey, limey. What's your name?'

'Bond. James Bond.'

'That's a pretty chump name. From England, huh?'

'That's right. Where's the registry? I'll spell it out for you.'

'Wise guy, huh? What's your line of business?'

'Police.'

Sluggsy's mouth opened. He ran his tongue over his lips. He

turned and called over to Horror, who was sitting at his old table, 'Hey, Horror. Guess what! This shamus is a limey dick! Whadya know about that? A gum-shoe!'

Horror nodded. 'Thought I smelled it. Who cares? We ain't done nuthin' wrong.'

'Yeh,' said Sluggsy eagerly, 'that's right too.' He turned to this Mr Bond. 'Now don't you go listening to any crap from this little hustler. We're from the insurance, see. Assessors, sort of. Work for Mr Sanguinetti. He's a big wheel in Troy. Owns this outfit. Well, there'd been complaints from the managers of some cash missing. Other things too. So we come up to make an investigation, sort of, and when we put the question to this little tramp she slams my friend with an ice-pick bang on the think-pot. See for yourself.' He waved in the direction of Horror. 'Now how d'ya like that? So we was just restraining her, sort of, when you comes along.' He turned. 'Ain't that right, Horror?'

'That's on the level. That's how it was.'

I said angrily, 'You know that's a pack of lies.' I walked over to the back door and pointed at the bent frame and the splash of lead. 'How did that bullet hole get there?'

Sluggsy laughed heartily. 'Search me, sister.' He turned to Horror. 'You seen any bullets flyin' around?'

'No, I ain't.' Horror's voice was bored. He waved a languid hand towards the floor round the eating counter. 'But I seen plenty hardware being slung at my pal by the lady.' His eyes swivelled slowly to me. 'That right, lady? An' there's a big carving knife down there somewhere. Good mind to book you for assault, come the morning.'

'You do that!' I said hotly. 'Just see where it'll get you! You know perfectly well I was trying to defend myself. And as for that story about the money, that's the first I've heard of it. And you know it.'

The Englishman broke in quietly. 'Well, it seems I came along at the right time to keep the peace. Now, where's that registry so that I can sign it.'

Sluggsy said curtly, 'Register's with de boss. No purpose in signin' nuthen. You ain't payin'. The place is closed. You can have your bed on the house.'

'Well, thanks. That's very kind of you.' James Bond turned to me. 'Any chance of some eggs and bacon and coffee? All this talking's made me hungry. I can cook it myself if the stuff's there.'

'Oh, no.' I almost ran behind the counter. 'I'd love to do it.'

'Thank you very much.' He turned his back on Sluggsy and sauntered over to the counter and hoisted himself on to a stool, putting his case on the next one.

Out of the corner of my eye I watched Sluggsy turn on his heel and walk quickly over to the thin man and sit down and begin talking urgently.

James Bond glanced over his shoulder at them and then got down off his stool and took off his raincoat and hat and put them on top of his case and climbed back. He silently watched the men in the long mirror at the back of the counter while I busied myself with the cooking things and took him in with quick glances.

He was about six feet tall, slim and fit-looking. The eyes in the lean, slightly tanned face were a very clear grey-blue and as they observed the men they were cold and watchful. The narrowed, watchful eyes gave his good looks the dangerous, almost cruel quality that had frightened me when I had first set eyes on him, but now that I knew how he could smile, I thought his face only exciting, in a way that no man's face had ever excited me before. He wore a soft-looking white silk shirt with a thin black knitted tie that hung down loosely without a pin, and his single-breasted suit was made of some dark blue lightweight material that may have been alpaca. The strong, rather good hands lay quietly on his crossed arms on the counter, and now he reached down to his hip pocket and took out a wide, thin gun-metal cigarette case and opened it.

'Have one? Senior Service. I suppose it'll have to be Chesterfields from now on.' His mouth turned slightly down as he smiled.

'No, thanks. Not now. After I've done the cooking.'

'By the way, what's your name? You're Canadian aren't you?'

'Yes, from Quebec. But I've been in England the last five years or so. I'm Vivienne Michel. My friends call me Viv.'

'How in God's name did you manage to get into this fix? Those are a couple of the toughest hoodlums I've seen in years. And Troy's a bad town—sort of a gangster suburb to Albany. The thin one's just finished a long stretch in jail, or I'll eat my hat. The other looks like the worst kind of psycho. How did it happen?'

I told him, in short bursts between the cooking, and cutting out all but the essentials. He listened quietly and without comment. Music was still coming from the radio, but the two gangsters were sitting silently watching us so I kept my voice low. When I had finished, I said, 'But is it true that you're a policeman?'

'Not quite. But I'm in that sort of business.'

'You mean a detective?'

'Well, sort of.'

'I knew it!'

He laughed. 'How?'

'Oh, I don't know. But you look, kind of, kind of dangerous. And that was a gun you took out of your bag, and ammunition. Are you'—I was embarrassed, but I needed to know—'are you official? I mean from the Government?'

He smiled reassuringly. 'Oh, yes. Don't worry about that.

And they know me in Washington. If we get out of this all right, I'm going to go after those two.' His eyes were cold again. 'I'm going to see they get roasted for what they did to you.'

'You believe me?'

'Of course. Every word. But what I can't make out is what they're up to. They seem to have acted as if they knew they were safe to do anything they liked with you. And now they seem quite calm about me having got into the act. I don't like it. Have they had any drinks? Do they smoke?'

'No. Neither of them.'

'I don't like that either. It's only pros that don't.'

I had finished cooking his supper and I put it up on the counter. He ate as if he was really hungry. I asked him if it was all right. He said it was wonderful and I felt warm inside. What a fantastic bit of luck this man, and just this man, coming so magically out of the blue! I felt humble about it. It was so much a miracle. I swore to myself to say my prayers that night, the first time for years. I hovered about him slavishly, offering him more coffee, some jam to finish his toast with. Finally he laughed tenderly at me, 'You're spoiling me. Here, I'm sorry. I forgot all about it. It's time for your cigarette. You've earned the whole caseful.' He lit it with a Ronson, gunmetalled like his case. My hand touched his and I felt a small shock pass down my body. I suddenly found I was trembling. I quickly took the dishes and began washing them. I said, 'I haven't earned anything. It's so wonderful you're here. It's an absolute miracle.' My voice choked and I felt stupid tears coming. I brushed the back of my hand across my eyes. He must have seen, but he pretended not to have.

Instead he said cheerfully, 'Yes. It was a stroke of luck. At least I hope so. Can't count the chickens yet. Tell you what. We've got to sit these two hoodlums out. Wait until they make a move, go to bed or something. Would you like to hear just how I came to turn up tonight? It'll all be in the papers in a day or two. The story. Only I won't be mentioned. So you must promise to forget my side of the thing. It's all nonsense, really. These regulations. But I have to work under them. All right? It might take your mind off your troubles. They seem to have been pretty powerful ones.'

I said gratefully, 'Yes, please tell me. And I promise. Cross my heart.'

11 / *BEDTIME STORY*

I hoisted myself up on to the drain board of the sink just beside him so that he could talk to me quietly—and so that I could be near to him. I refused another cigarette, and he lit one and gazed for a long minute into the mirror watching the two gangsters. I looked, too. The two men just stared back with a passive, indifferent hostility that seeped steadily across the room like poison gas. I didn't much like their indifference and their watchfulness. It seemed so powerful, so implacable, as if the odds were on their side and they had all the time in the world. But this James Bond didn't seem worried. He just seemed to be weighing them up, like a chess player. There was a certitude of power, of superiority, in his eyes that worried me. He hadn't seen these men in action. He couldn't possibly know what they were capable of, how at any moment they might just blaze away with their guns, blowing our heads off like coconuts in a circus sideshow, and then toss our bodies in the lake with stones to keep them down. But then James Bond began talking, and I forgot my nightmares and just watched his face and listened.

'In England,' he said, 'when a man, or occasionally a woman, comes over from the other side, from the Russian side, with important information, there's a fixed routine. Take Berlin, for instance, and that's the most usual come-over route. To begin with they get taken to intelligence headquarters and get treated at first with extra suspicion. That's to try and take care of double agents—people who pretend to come over and, once they've been cleared by security, begin spying on us from inside, so to speak, and pass their stuff back to the Russians. There are also triple agents—people who do what the doubles have done, but change their minds and, under our control, pass phoney intelligence back to the Russians. Do you understand? It's nothing but a complicated game, really. But then so's international politics, diplomacy—all the trappings of nationalism and the power complex that goes on between countries. Nobody will stop playing the game. It's like the hunting instinct.'

'Yes, I see. It all seems idiotic to my generation. Like playing that old game "Attaque", really. We need some more Jack Kennedys. It's all these old people about. They ought to hand the world over to younger people who haven't got the idea of war stuck in their subconscious. As if it were the only solution. Like beating children. It's much the same thing. It's all out of date—Stone Age stuff.'

He smiled. 'As a matter of fact I agree, but don't spread your ideas too widely or I'll find myself out of a job. Anyway, once the come-over has got through the strainer in Berlin, he's flown to England and the bargain gets made—you tell us all you know about the Russian rocket sites and in exchange we'll give you a new name, a British passport and a hideout where the Russians will never find you. That's what they're most frightened of, of course, the Russians getting after them and killing them. And, if they play, they get the choice of Canada, Australia, New Zealand or Africa. So, when they've told all they know, they get flown out to the country they've chosen, and there a reception committee run by the local police, a very hush-hush affair, of course, takes them over and they're gradually eased into a job and into a community just as if they were a bona fide immigrant. It nearly always works all right. They get homesick to begin with, and have trouble settling down, but some member of the reception committee will always be at hand to give them any help they need.'

James Bond lit another cigarette. 'I'm not telling you anything the Russians don't know. The only secret side of the business is the addresses of these people. There's a man I'll call Boris. He's been settled in Canada, in Toronto. He was a prize—twenty-four carat. He was a top naval constructor in Kronstadt—high up in their nuclear submarine team. He got away to Finland and then to Stockholm. We picked him up and flew him to England. The Russians don't often say anything about their defectors—just curse and let them go. If they're important, they round up their families and ship them off to Siberia—to frighten other waverers. But it was different with Boris. They sent out a general call to their secret services to eliminate him. As luck would have it, an organization called SPECTRE somehow listened in.'

James Bond took a hard look at the two men on the other side of the room. They hadn't moved. They sat there and watched and waited. What for? James Bond turned back to me. 'I'm not boring you?'

'Oh, no. Of course not. It's thrilling. These SPECTRE people. Haven't I read about them somewhere? In the papers?'

'I expect you have. Less than a year ago there was this business of the stolen atomic bombs. It was called Operation *Thunderball*. Remember?' His eyes went far away. 'It was in the Bahamas.'

'Oh, yes. Of course I remember. It was in all the papers. I could hardly believe it. It was like something out of a thriller. Why? Were you mixed up in it?'

James Bond smiled. 'On the sidelines. But the point is that

we never cleaned up SPECTRE. The top man got away. It was a kind of independent spy network—"The Special Executive for Counter-espionage, Terrorism, Revenge and Extortion" they call themselves. Well, they've got going again and, as I say, they came to hear that the Russians wanted Boris killed and somehow they found out where he was. Don't ask me how. These people are too damned well informed for comfort. So they put it to the top KGB man in Paris, the local head of the Russian Secret Service, that they'd do the job for one hundred thousand pounds. Presumably Moscow agreed, because the next thing that happened was that Ottawa—the famous Mounties—got on to us. They have a Special Branch that we work with pretty closely on this sort of thing, and they reported that there was an ex-Gestapo man in Toronto, chap called Horst Uhlmann, making contact with the gangs there, and did we know anything about him? It seemed he wanted some unspecified foreigner bumped off and was prepared to pay fifty thousand dollars for the job. Well, two and two got put together and some bright chap in our show had a hunch this might be an attempt on Boris by the Russians. 'So,' James Bond's mouth curled down, 'I was sent out to look into the business.'

He smiled at me. 'You wouldn't rather switch on the television?'

'Oh, no. Go on please.'

'Well, you know they've been having a lot of trouble in Toronto. It's anyway a tough town, but now gang war has broken out in a big way, and you probably read that the Mounties even went so far as to call in two top CID sleuths from Scotland Yard to help them out. One of these CID chaps had managed to plant a smart young Canadian in "The Mechanics", which is the name of the toughest Toronto gang, with affiliations over the border with Chicago and Detroit. And it was this young man who got wind of Uhlmann and what he wanted done. Well, I and my Mountie pals went to work and to cut a long story short we found out that it *was* Boris who was the target and that The Mechanics had agreed to do the job last Thursday—that's just about a week ago. Uhlmann had gone to ground and we couldn't get a smell of him. All we could discover from our man with The Mechanics was that he had agreed to lead the murder squad that was to consist of three top gunmen from the mob. It was to be a frontal attack on the apartment where Boris lived. Nothing fancy. They were just going to blast their way through the front door with sub-machine-guns, shoot him to bits, and get away. It was to be at night, just before midnight, and The Mechanics would mount a permanent watch on the apartment house to see that Boris came home from his job and didn't go out again.

'Well, apart from protecting Boris, my main job was to get this Horst Uhlmann, because by now we were as certain as could be that he was a SPECTRE man, and one of my jobs is to go after these people wherever they show up. Of course, we couldn't leave Boris in danger, but if we got him away to safety there would be no attempt on his life and so no Uhlmann. So I had to make a rather unpleasant suggestion.' James Bond smiled grimly. 'Unpleasant for me, that is. From his photographs, I had noticed that there was a superficial resemblance between Boris and me—about my age, tall, dark, clean-shaven so I took a look at him from a ghost car one day—that's an undercover prowl car—and watched how he walked and what he wore. Then I suggested that we get Boris away on the day before the murder job, and that I should take his place on the last walk back to his apartment.'

I couldn't help saying anxiously, 'Oh, but you shouldn't have taken the risk. Supposing they'd changed the plan. Supposing they'd decided to do it as you walked down the street, or with a time bomb or something!'

He shrugged. 'We thought of all that. It was a calculated risk and it's those I'm paid for taking.' He smiled. 'Anyway, here I am. But it wasn't nice walking down that street, and I was glad to get inside. The Mounties had taken over the flat opposite to Boris and I knew I was all right and simply had to play the tethered goat while the sportsmen shot the wild game. I could have stayed out of the flat, hidden somewhere in the building until it was all over, but I had a hunch that the goat must be a real goat, and I was right, because at eleven o'clock the telephone rang and a man's voice said, "Is that Mr Boris?" giving his assumed name. I said, "Yes. Who is dat?" trying to sound foreign, and the man said, "Thank you. Telephone Directory here. We're just checking the subscribers in your district. 'Night." I said goodnight and thanked my stars I had been there to take the bogus call that was to make sure Boris was at home.

'The last hour was nervous work. There was going to be a lot of gunfire and probably a lot of death, and no one likes the prospect of those things even if they don't expect to be hit. I had a couple of guns, heavy ones that really stop people, and at ten to twelve I took up my position to the right of the door in an angle of solid masonry and got ready just in case Uhlmann or one of the hoodlums managed to bust through the Mounties across the passage. To tell you the truth, as the minutes went by and I could imagine the killer car coming down the street and the men piling out and running softly up the stairs, I wished I had accepted the Mounties' offer that one of their men should share this vigil, as they called it, with me. But it would have been a five-hour *tête-à-tête* and, apart from not knowing what we would talk about during all that time, I've always had a preference for operating alone. It's just the way I'm made. Well, the minutes and the seconds ticked by and then, bang on time, at five minutes to midnight, I heard a rush of rubber soles on the stairs and then all hell broke loose.'

James Bond paused. He rubbed a hand down over his face. It was a gesture that was either to clear his mind's eye or to try and wipe some memory away from it. Then he lit another cigarette and went on.

'I heard the lieutenant in charge of the Mountie party shout, "It's the law! Get 'em up!" And then there was a mixture of single shots and bursts from the chopper'—he grinned—'sorry, sub-machine-gun—and somebody screamed. Then the lieutenant shouted, "Get that man!" and the next moment the lock blew off the door beside me and a man charged in. He held a smoking machine-gun tight against the hip, which is the way to use them, and he whirled from right to left in the bedsitter looking for Boris. I knew it was Uhlmann, the ex-Gestapo man. One's had to get to know the smell of a German, and of a Russian for the matter of that, in my line of work, and I had him in my sights. I shot at his gun and blasted it out of his hands. But he was quick. He jumped behind the open door. The door was only a thin bit of wood. I couldn't take a chance on him having another gun and firing first, so I sprayed a wide Z of bullets through the wood, bending my knees lower as I did so. Just as well I did this, because he fired a quick burst that nearly parted my hair when I was almost on my knees. But two of my bullets had got him, in the left shoulder and right hip as it turned out, and he crashed down behind the door and lay quiet.

'The rest of the battle outside had disappeared down the stairs after the gunmen, but a wounded Mountie suddenly appeared at the entrance to my room on hands and knees to help me. He said, "Want a hand, feller?" and Uhlmann fired through the door at the voice and . . . and, well, he killed the man. But that gave me the height of Uhlmann's gun and I fired almost as he did, and then I ran out into the centre of the room to give him some more if need be. But he didn't need any more. He was still alive, and when the remains of the Mounties came back up the stairs, we took him down and into an ambulance and tried to get him to talk in hospital. But he wouldn't—a mixture of Gestapo and SPECTRE is a good one—and he died the next morning.'

James Bond looked me in the eyes, but his own didn't see me. He said, 'We lost two of our side and another wounded. They lost the German, and one of theirs, and the other two won't last long. But the battlefield was a nasty sight and, well,' his face looked suddenly drawn and tired, 'I've seen enough of this sort of thing. After the various post-mortems were over I wanted to get away. My headquarters, and the Mounties backed them up, wanted me to report the whole case to Washington, to our opposite numbers there, to get their help in cleaning up the American end of The Mechanics gang. The Mechanics had been given a nasty jolt, and the Mounties Special Branch thought it would be a good idea to follow up while they were still groggy. I said all right, but that I would like to drive down and not just dash off in an aeroplane or train. That was allowed so long as I didn't take more than three days and I hired this car and started at dawn this morning. I was going all right, pretty fast, when I ran into the hell of a storm, the tail of yours I suppose. I got through it as far as Lake George and I meant to stay the night there, but it looked such a hellish place that when I saw a sign up at a side road advertising this motel I took a chance.' He smiled at me, and now he looked quite cheerful again. 'Perhaps something told me you were at the end of the road and that you were in trouble. Anyway, I had a puncture a mile from here, and here I am.' He smiled again, and reached out and put his hand on mine on the counter. 'Funny the way things work out!'

'But you must be absolutely beat, driving all that way.'

'I've got something for that. Be a good girl and give me another cup of coffee.'

While I busied myself with the percolator, he opened his case and took out a small bottle of white pills. He took out two and when I gave him the coffee he swallowed them down. 'Benzedrine. That'll keep me awake for tonight. I'll fit in some sleep tomorrow.' His eyes went to the mirror. 'Hullo. Here they come.' He gave me a smile of encouragement. 'Now just don't worry. Get some sleep. I'll be around to see there's no trouble.'

The music on the radio faded and musical chimes sounded midnight.

12 / *TO SLEEP—PERCHANCE TO DIE!*

While Sluggsy made for the back door and went out into the night, the thin man came slowly over to us. He leaned against the edge of the counter. 'Okay, folks. Break it up. It's midnight. We're turning off the electricity. My friend's getting emergency oil-lamps from the storehouse. No sense wasting juice. Mr Sanguinetti's orders.' The words were friendly and reasonable. Had they decided to give up their plans, whatever they were, because of this man Bond? I doubted it. The thoughts that listening to James Bond's story had driven away came flooding back. I was going to have to sleep with these two men in the adjoining cabins on both sides of me. I *must* make my room impregnable. But they had the pass-key! I must get this man Bond to help me.

James Bond yawned hugely. 'Well, I'll certainly be glad of some sleep. Came a long way today and I've got plenty more to cover tomorrow. And you must be ready for bed, too, with all your worries.'

'Come again, mister?' The thin man's eyes had sharpened.

'It's a pretty responsible job you've got.'

'What job's that?'

'Oh, being an insurance assessor. On a valuable property like this. Must be worth half a million dollars, I'd say. By the way, are either of you bonded?'

'No, we ain't. Mr Sanguinetti don't need to bond no one what works for him.'

'That's a great compliment to his staff. Must have good men. Quite right to put a lot of trust in them. Incidentally, what's the name of his insurance company?'

'Metro Accident and Home.' The thin man still leaned relaxed against the counter, but the grey face was now tense. 'Why? What's it to you, mister? Suppose you quit with the double-talk and say what's on your mind.'

Bond said carelessly, 'Miss Michel here was telling me the motel hadn't been doing so well. I gather the place hasn't been accepted for membership in Quality Courts or Holiday Inns or Congress. Difficult to do much trade without one of those affiliations. And all this trouble to send up you fellows to count the spoons and turn off the electric light and so on.' James Bond looked sympathetic. 'Just crossed my mind that the business might be on the rocks. Too bad if it is. Nice set-up here, and a fine site.'

The red fleck that I had seen once, terribly, before was now in the thin man's eyes. He said softly, 'Just suppose you bag your lip, mister. I ain't standin' for no more limey cracks, get me? You suggestin' this ain't legit? Mebbe you think we set one up, huh?'

'Now don't burn yourself up, Mr Horowitz. No need to sing the weeps.' James Bond smiled broadly. 'You see I know the lingo, too.' His smile suddenly went. 'And I also know where it comes from. Now, do *you* get *me*?'

I suppose he meant this was gangster, jailbird language. The thin man certainly thought so. He looked startled, but now he had conquered his anger and he just said, 'Okay, wise guy. I've got the photo. You gum-shoes are all the same—looking for dirt where there ain't none. Now, where in hell's that pal of mine? C'mon. Let's hit the pad.'

As we filed out through the back door, the lights went out. James Bond and I stopped, but the thin man went on along the covered way as if he could see in the dark. Sluggsy appeared round the corner of the building carrying two oil-lamps. He handed one to each of us. His naked face, yellow in the light, split into a grin. 'Happy dreams, folks!'

James Bond followed me over to my cabin and came inside. He shut the door. 'Damned if I know what they're up to, but the first thing to do is see that you're properly closed down for the night. Now then, let's see.' He prowled round the room, examining the window fastenings, inspecting the hinges on the door, estimating the size of the ventilator louvres. He seemed satisfied. He said, 'There's only the door. You say they've got the master key. We'll wedge the door, and when I've gone just move the desk over as an extra barricade.' He went into the bathroom, tore off strips of lavatory paper, moistened them and made them into firm wedges. He rammed several under the door, turned the handle and pulled. They held, but could have been shaken loose by ramming. He took the wedges out again and gave them to me. Then he put his hand to the belt of his trousers and took out a short, stumpy revolver. 'Ever fired one of these things?'

I said I'd shot at rabbits with a long-barrelled .22 target pistol when I was young.

'Well, this is a Smith and Wesson Police Positive. A real stopper. Remember to aim low. Hold your arm out straight like this.' He showed me. 'And try to squeeze the trigger and not snatch at it. But it won't really matter. I'll hear it and I'll come running. Now remember. You've got absolute protection. The windows are good solid stuff and there's no way of getting in between the glass slats, short of smashing them.' He smiled. 'Trust these motel designers. They know all there is to know about break-ins. These hoodlums won't take a shot at you through them in the dark, but, just in case, leave your bed where it is and make up a camp bed with some cushions and bedding in that far corner on the floor. Put the gun under your pillow. Pull the desk in front of the door and balance the television set on the edge of it so that if anyone barges the door they knock it off. That'll wake you and then you just fire a shot through the door, close to the handle, where the man will be standing, and listen for the squawk. Got it?'

I said yes, as happily as I could, and wished he would stay in the room with me. But I hadn't the guts to ask him, and anyway he seemed to have his own plans.

He came up to me and kissed me gently on the lips. I was so surprised I just stood there. He said lightly, 'I'm sorry, Viv, but you're a beautiful girl. In those overalls you're the prettiest garage-hand I've ever seen. Now don't you worry. Get some sleep. I'll keep an eye on you.'

I threw my arms round his neck and kissed him back—hard, on the lips. I said, 'You're the most wonderful man I've ever met in my life. Thank you for being here. And please, James. Be careful! You haven't seen them like I have. They're really tough. Please don't get hurt.'

He kissed me back, but only lightly, and I let go of him. He said, 'Don't worry. I've seen this sort before. Now you do all I told you and get off to sleep. 'Night, Viv.'

And then he had gone.

I stood for a moment looking at the closed door, and then I went and brushed my teeth and got ready for bed. I looked at myself in the mirror. I looked like hell—washed out, no make-up, and deep circles under my eyes. What a day! And now this! I mustn't lose him! I mustn't let him go! But I knew in my heart that I had to. He would go on alone and I would have to, too. No woman had ever held this man. None ever would. He was a solitary, a man who walked alone and kept his heart to himself. He would hate involvement. I sighed. All right. I would play it that way. I would let him go. I wouldn't cry when he did. Not even afterwards. Wasn't I the girl who had decided to operate without a heart?

Silly idiot! Silly, infatuated goose! This was a fine time to maunder like a girl in a woman's magazine! I shook my head angrily and went into the bedroom and got on with what I had to do.

It was still blowing hard and the pine trees clashed fiercely outside my back window. The moon, filtering through high scudding clouds, lit up the two high squares of glass at each end of the room and shone eerily through the thin, red-patterned curtains. When the moon went behind the clouds, the blocks of blood-red photographer's light went dark and there was only the meagre pool of yellow from the oil-lamp. Without the brightness of electricity, there was a nasty little movie-set feeling about the oblong room. The corners were dark and the room seemed to be waiting for a director to call people out of the shadows and tell them what to do.

I tried not to be nervous. I put my ears to the connecting walls to right and left, but across the space of the car-ports I could hear nothing. Before I had set up my barricade I had softly opened the door and gone out and looked round. There had been a glimmer of light from Numbers 8 and 10 and from James Bond's Number 40 away down to the left. Everything had been peaceful, everything quiet. Now I stood in the middle of the room and had a last look round. I had done everything he had told me to do. I remembered the prayers I was going to say and I knelt down there and then on the carpet and said them. I thanked, but I also asked. Then I took two aspirin, turned down the light and blew across the glass chimney to put it out, and went over to my floor bed in the corner. After unzipping the front of my overalls and unlacing but not removing my shoes, I curled myself up in the blankets.

I never take aspirins or any other pills. These, after carefully reading the instructions, I had taken from the little first-aid kit my practical mind had told me to include in my scrap of luggage. I was anyway exhausted, beat to the wide, and the pills, to me as strong as morphia, soon sent me off into a delicious half-sleep in which there was no danger but only the dark, exciting face and the new-found knowledge that there really did exist such men. Soppier even than that, I remembered the first touch of his hand holding the lighter and thought carefully about each kiss separately, and then, but only after vaguely remembering the gun and slipping my hand under the pillow to make sure it was there, I went happily to sleep.

The next thing I knew I was wide awake. I lay for a moment remembering where I was. There was a lull in the wind and it was very quiet. I found I was lying on my back. That was what had awakened me! I lay for a moment looking across the room at the square of red high up on the opposite wall. The moon was out again. How deathly quiet it was! The silence was warm and embracing after the hours of storm. I began to feel drowsy and I turned over on my side so that I lay facing into the room. I closed my eyes. But, as sleep held out her hands to me again, something nagged at my mind. My eyes, before I had closed them, had noticed something unusual in the room. Unwillingly, I opened them again. It took minutes to recognize again what I had seen. The faintest chinks of light were shining from between the door frames of the clothes cupboard up against the opposite wall.

How stupid! I hadn't closed the doors properly and the automatic 'courtesy' light inside hadn't switched itself off. Reluctantly I got out of bed. What a bore! And then, after I had taken only two steps across the room, I suddenly remembered. But there wouldn't be a light inside the cupboard! The electricity was switched off!

I stood for a moment, my hand up to my mouth, and then, as I turned to dive for the gun, the doors of the cupboard burst open and the crouching figure of Sluggsy darted out and, a flashlight in one hand and something swinging from the other, he was on top of me.

I think I gave a shrill scream, but perhaps it was only within me. The next moment something exploded against the side of my head and I felt myself crash to the floor. Then all was darkness.

My first sensations on coming round were of terrific heat and of being dragged along the ground. Then I smelled the burning and saw the flames and I tried to scream. I realized that nothing was coming out of my mouth but an animal whimpering, and I began to kick with my feet. But the hands held my ankles firmly and then suddenly, with painful bumps that added to the frightful pain in my head, I found myself being dragged into wet grass and tree branches. Suddenly my feet were laid down and there was a man on his knees beside me and his firm hand over my mouth. A voice close to my ear, James Bond's voice, whispered urgently, 'Don't make a sound! Lie still! It's all right. It's me.'

I put a hand out to him and felt his shoulder. It was naked. I pressed it to reassure him and the hand came away from my mouth. He whispered, 'Wait there! Don't move! Be back in a second,' and he slipped noiselessly away.

Noiselessly? It wouldn't have mattered how much noise he made. There was a tremendous roar and crackle of flames behind me and orange light flickered against the trees. I got carefully to my knees and painfully turned my head. A great wall of flame extended down to my right all along the row of cabins. God, what he had saved me from! I felt my body and put my hands up to my hair. I was untouched. There was only the throbbing bruise at the back of my head. I found I could stand, and I got up and tried to think what had happened. But I could remember nothing after I had got hit. So they must have set fire to the place and James had somehow got to me in time and pulled me out into the trees at the back!

There was a rustle among the trees and he was beside me. He was wearing no shirt or coat, but there was some kind of harness across the sunburned, sweating chest that glistened in the light of the flames, and a heavy-looking automatic hung, butt down, below his left armpit. His eyes were bright with tension and excitement and his smoke-streaked face and tousled hair made him look piratical and rather frightening.

He smiled grimly. He nodded in the direction of the flames. 'That's the game. Burn the place down for the insurance. They're just fixing the flames to reach the lobby building, sprinkling thermite dust along the covered way. I couldn't care less. If I took them on now, I'd only be saving Mr Sanguinetti's property for him. With us as witnesses, he won't even smell the insurance. And he'll be in jail. So we'll just wait a bit and let him have a total loss on his books.'

I suddenly thought of my precious belongings. I said humbly, 'Can we save the Vespa?'

'It's all right. You've only lost those glad-rags—if you left them in the bathroom. I got the gun when I got you, and I slung the saddle-bags out. I've just been salvaging the Vespa. It looks in good shape. I've made a cache of everything in the trees. Those car-ports will be the last things to go. They've got masonry on both sides. They've used thermite bombs in each of the cabins. Better than petrol. Less bulky and they leave no traces for the insurance sleuths.'

'But you might have got burned!'

His smile flashed white in the shadows. 'That's why I took my coat off. I must look respectable in Washington.'

It didn't seem funny to me. 'But what about your shirt?'

There was a crash and a great shower of sparks way down the line of cabins. James Bond said, 'There goes my shirt. Roof falling in on top of it.' He paused and wiped his hand down his dirty sweating face so that the black smudged even worse. 'I had a feeling something like this was going to happen. Perhaps I should have been more ready for it than I was. I could have gone and changed the wheel on my car, for instance. If I'd done that we could get out now. We could work our way round the end of the cabins and make a dash for it. Get to Lake George or Glens Falls and send the cops along. But I thought that if I fixed the car our friends would have an excuse to tell me to get moving. I could have refused, of course, or said that I wouldn't go without you, but I thought that might lead to shooting. I'd be lucky to beat those two unless I shot first. And with me out of the picture, you'd have been back where we started. That would have been bad. You were a major part of their plan.'

'I felt I was all along. I didn't know why. I knew the way they were treating me meant that I didn't matter, that I was expendable. What did they want to use me for?'

'You were to have been the cause of the fire. The evidence for Sanguinetti would have been that the managers, this Phancey couple, and of course they're in it up to their necks,'—I remembered the way their attitude to me had changed on the last day; the way they too had treated me with contempt, as rubbish, as something that was to be thrown away—'they would say that they had told you to turn off the electricity—perfectly reasonable as the place was closing down—and use an oil-lamp for the last night. The remains of the oil-lamp would have been found. You had gone to sleep with the light on and somehow upset it. The whole place blazed up and that was that. The buildings had a lot of timber in them and the wind did the rest. My turning-up was a nuisance, but not more than that. My remains would have been found too—or at any rate my car and wrist watch and the metal from my bag. I don't know what they'd have done about my gun and the one under your pillow. Those might have got them into trouble. The police would have checked the car with Canada and then the numbers of the guns with England and that would have identified me. So why was my other gun under your pillow? That might have made the police think. If we were, well, sort of lovers, why was I sleeping so far away from you? Perhaps we had both been very proper and slept as far apart as possible and I had insisted that you have one of my guns to protect a lonely girl in the night. I don't know how they would have worked it out. But my guess is that our friends, once I told them I was a policeman, may have thought about guns and other incriminating hardware that wouldn't be destroyed in the fire and might have waited a few hours and then gone in and raked about in the ashes to take care of that sort of trouble. They'd have been careful about their raking, and of their footprints in the cinders, of course. But then these people are pros.' His mouth turned down. 'By their standards, that is.'

'But why didn't they kill you?'

'They did, or rather they thought they had. When I left you and went along to my cabin, I reckoned that if anything was going to happen to you they would get rid of me first. So I rigged up a dummy in my bed. A good one. I've done it before and I've got the trick. You mustn't only have something that looks like a body in the bed. You can do that with pillows and towels and bedding. You must also have something that looks like hair on the pillow. I did that with handfuls of pine needles, just enough to make a dark clump on the pillow with the sheets drawn up to it—very artistic. Then I hung my shirt over the back of a chair beside the bed—another useful prop that conveys the idea that the man belonging to the shirt is inside the bed—and I left the oil-lamp burning low, close to the bed to help their marksmanship—if any. I put amateurish wedges under the door and propped a chair-back under the door handle to show a natural sense of precaution. Then I took my bag round to the back and waited in the trees.' James Bond gave a sour laugh. 'They gave me an hour and then they came so softly that I didn't hear a thing. Then there was the bang of the door being forced and a series of quick clonks—they were using a silencer—and then the whole interior of the cabin went bright with the thermite. I thought I had been very clever, but it turned out I very nearly wasn't clever enough. It took me almost five minutes to work my way up to your cabin through the trees. I wasn't worried. I thought it would take them all that to get into your cabin and I was ready to break out in the open if I heard your gun. But some time this evening, probably when Sluggsy was making the cabin inspection you told me about, he had pick-axed a hole in the wall behind your clothes cupboard, leaving only the plaster-board lining to be cut through with a sharp knife. He may or may not have put the stone loosely back. I don't know. Anyway, he didn't need to. There was no occasion for either of us to go into the car-port of Number 8, and no reason to. If you had been here alone, they would have seen to it that you kept away from there. Anyway, the first thing I knew was seeing the light of the thermite from your cabin. Then I ran like hell, dodging across the open back of the car-ports as I heard them coming back down the line, opening the doors of the cabins and tossing bombs in and then carefully shutting the doors to make it look tidy.'

During all this while, James Bond had been glancing from time to time at the roof of the lobby building that we could just see over the tops of the flaming cabins. Now he said casually, 'They've set it going. I'll have to get after them. How are you feeling, Viv? Any stuffing left? How's the head?'

I said impatiently, 'Oh, I'm all right. But James, do you have to go after them? Let them get away. What do they matter? You might get hurt.'

He said firmly, 'No, darling. They almost killed both of us. Any minute now they may come back and find the Vespa gone. Then we'll have lost the surprise factor. And I can't let them get away with it. These are killers. They'll be off killing someone else tomorrow.' He smiled cheerfully. 'Besides, they ruined my shirt!'

'Well, then you must let me help.' I put my hand out to him. 'And you will take care, won't you? I can't do without you. I don't want to be alone again.'

He ignored my hand. He said, almost coldly, 'Now don't hang on my gun arm, there's a good girl. This is something I've got to do. It's just a job. Now,' he handed me the Smith and Wesson, 'you move quietly up in the trees to the car-port of Number 3. That's in the dark and the wind's blowing the fire the other way. You can watch from there without being seen. If I need help, I'll know where to find you, so don't budge. If I call, come running fast. If anything happens to me, get moving along the shore of the lake and work your way as far as you can. After this fire, there'll be plenty of police along tomorrow, and you can smuggle yourself back and contact one of them. They'll believe you. If they argue, tell them to ring up CIA in Washington, the Central Intelligence Agency, and you'll see plenty of action. Just say who I was. I've got a number in my outfit—sort of recognition number. It's 007. Try not to forget it.'

13 / *THE CRASH OF GUNS*

'I *was*.' 'Say who I *was* . . .'

Why did he have to say such a thing, put the idea into the mind of God, of Fate, of whoever was controlling tonight? One should never send out black thoughts. They live on, like sound-waves, and get into the stream of consciousness in which we all swim. If God, Fate, happened to be listening in, at that moment, on that particular wave-length, it might be made to happen. The hint of a death-thought might be misunderstood. It might be read as a request!

So I mustn't think these thoughts either, or I would be adding my weight to the dark waves of destiny! What nonsense! I had learned this sort of stuff from Kurt. He had always been full of 'cosmic chain reactions', 'cryptograms of the life-force' and other Germanic magical double-talk that I had avidly lapped up as if, as he had sometimes hinted, he himself had been the 'Central Dynamic', or at least part of it, who controlled all these things.

Of course James Bond had said that flippantly, in a cross-my-fingers way, like the skiers I had known in Europe who said *'Hals und Beinbruch!'* to their friends before they took off on the slalom or the downhill race. To wish them 'Break your neck and your leg' before the off was to avert accidents, to invoke the opposite of the evil eye. James Bond was just being

'British'—using a throwaway phrase to buck me up. Well, I wished he hadn't. The crash of guns, gangsters, attempted murders, were part of his job, his life. They weren't part of mine, and I blamed him for not being more sensitive, more human.

Where was he now? Working his way through the shadows, using the light of the flames as cover, pricking up his senses for danger? And what were the enemy doing? Those two pro gangsters he was too quick to despise? Were they waiting for him in ambush? Would there suddenly be a roar of gunfire? Then screams?

I got to the car-port of Number 3 cabin and, brushing along the rough-cast stone wall, felt my way through the darkness. I cautiously inched the last few feet and looked round the corner towards the dancing flames and shadows of the other cabins and of the lobby block.

There was no one to be seen, no movement except the flames at which the wind tugged intermittently to keep the blaze alive. Now some of the bordering trees behind the cabins were almost catching and sparks were blowing from their drying branches away into the darkness. If it hadn't been for the storm, surely a forest fire would have been started and then the coshed girl with her broken lamp would indeed have left her mark on the United States of America! How far would it have gone with the wind to help it? Ten miles? Twenty? How many trees and birds and animals would the little dead girl from Quebec have destroyed?

Another cabin roof fell in and there was the same great shower of orange sparks. And now the gimcrack timbered roof of the lobby block was going. It caved slowly inwards and then collapsed like a badly-cooked soufflé, and more showers of sparks went up gaily and burned themselves out as they briefly drifted away on the wind. The extra burst of flame showed up the two cars beside the road, the grey Thunderbird and the shining black sedan. But there was still no sign of the gangsters and none of James Bond.

I suddenly realized that I had forgotten all about time. I looked at my watch. It was two o'clock. So it was only five hours since all this had begun! It could have been weeks. My former life seemed almost years away. Even last evening, when I had sat and thought about that life, was difficult to remember. Everything had suddenly been erased. Fear and pain and danger had taken over. It was like being in a shipwreck, an aeroplane- or a train-crash, an earthquake or a hurricane. When these things happen to you, it must be just the same. The black wings of emergency blot out the sky and there is no past and no future. You live through each minute, survive each second, as though it is your last. There is no other time, no other place, but now and here.

And then I saw the men! They were coming up towards me on the grass, and each was carrying a big box in his hands. They were television sets. They must have salvaged them to sell and make themselves a little extra cash. They walked side by side, the thin man and the squat, and the light from the flaming cabins shone on their sweating faces. When they came to the charred arches of the covered way to the lobby block, they trotted quickly through, after glancing up at the still-burning roof to make sure it wouldn't fall on them. Where was James Bond? This was the perfect time to get them, with their hands full!

Now they were only twenty yards away from me, veering right towards their car. I cringed back into the dark cave of the car-port. But where was James? Should I run out after them and take them on alone? Don't be idiotic! If I missed, and I certainly would, that would be the end of me. Now, if they turned round, would they see me? Would my white overalls show up in the darkness? I got farther back. Now they were framed in the square opening of my car-port as they walked across the grass a few yards from the still-standing north wall of the lobby building from which the wind had so far kept most of the flames. They would soon vanish round the corner and a wonderful chance would have gone!

And then they stopped, stockstill, and there was James facing them, his gun aiming dead steady between the two bodies! His voice cracked like a whip across the lawn. 'All right! This is it! Turn round! The first man drops his television gets shot.'

They turned slowly round so that they faced towards my hideout. And now James called to me, 'Come over, Viv! I need extra hands.'

I took the heavy revolver out of the waistband of my overalls and ran quickly across the grass. When I was about ten yards from the men, James said, 'Just stop there, Viv, and I'll tell you what to do.' I stopped. The two evil faces stared at me. The thin man's teeth were bared in a sort of fixed grin of surprise and tension. Sluggsy let off a string of curses. I pointed my gun at the television set that covered his stomach. 'Shut your mouth or I'll shoot you dead.'

Sluggsy sneered. 'You and who else? You'd be too frightened of the bang.'

James said, 'Shut up you, or you get a crack on that ugly head of yours. Now listen, Viv, we've got to get the guns off these men. Come round behind the one called Horror. Put your gun up against his spine and with your free hand feel under his armpits. Not a nice job but it can't be helped. Tell me if you feel a gun there and I'll tell you what to do next. We'll go at this slowly. I'll cover the other, and if this Horror moves let him have it.'

I did as I was told. I went round behind the thin man and pressed the gun into his back. Then I reached up with my left hand and felt under his right arm. A nasty, dead kind of smell came from him, and I was suddenly disgusted at being so close to him and touching him so intimately.

I know that my hand trembled, and it must have been that that made him take the chance, for, suddenly, in one quick flow of motion, he had dropped the television, whirled like a snake, slapping the gun out of my hand with his open palm, and clutched me to him.

James Bond's gun roared and I felt the wind of a bullet, and then I began to fight like a demon, kicking and scratching and clawing. But I might have been fighting with a stone statue. He just squeezed me more agonizingly to him and I heard his dry voice say, 'Okay, limey. Now what? Want the dame to get herself killed?'

I could feel one of his hands loosening itself from me to get to his gun and I began struggling again.

James Bond said sharply, 'Viv. Get your legs apart!'

I automatically did as I was told and again his gun roared. The thin man let out a curse and set me free, but at the same time there came a splintering crash from behind me and I whirled round. At the same time as he had fired, Sluggsy had hurled the television set over his head at James Bond and it had crashed into his face, knocking him off balance.

As Sluggsy shouted, 'Scram, Horror!' I dived for my gun and, prone in the grass, clumsily fired it at Sluggsy. I would probably have missed him anyway, but he was already on the move, weaving across the lawn towards the cabins like a football player, with the thin man scrambling desperately after him. I fired again, but the gun kicked high, and then they were out of range and Sluggsy disappeared into Number 1 cabin away on the right.

I got up and ran to James Bond. He was kneeling down in the grass with one hand to his head. As I came up he took the hand away, looked at it and swore. There was a big gash just below the hairline. I didn't say anything, but ran to the nearest window of the lobby building and smashed it in with the butt of my gun. A burst of heat came out at me, but no flames, and, just below, almost within reach, was the table the gangsters had used, and on it, among some smouldering remains of the roof, the first-aid kit. James Bond shouted something, but I was already over the sill. I held my breath against the fumes, grabbed the box and scrambled out again, my eyes stinging with the smoke.

I wiped the wound as clean as I could, and got out merthiolate and a big Band-aid. The cut wasn't deep, but there would soon be a bad bruise. He said, 'Sorry, Viv. I made rather a hash of that round.'

I thought he had too. I said, 'Why didn't you just shoot them down? They were sitting ducks with those sets in their hands.'

He said curtly, 'Never been able to in cold blood. But at least I ought to have been able to blast that man's foot off. Must have just nicked it, and now he's still in the game.'

I said severely, 'It seems to me damned lucky you're in it too. Why didn't Sluggsy kill you?'

'Your guess is as good as mine. It looks as if they've got some kind of a headquarters over at Number 1. Perhaps he left his armament there while they did the job on the lobby. He may not have liked carrying live bullets around with him so near to the flames. Anyway, war's declared now, and we're going to have quite a job on our hands. Main thing is to keep an eye on their car. They'll be pretty desperate to get away. But they've somehow got to kill us first. They're in a nasty fix and they'll fight like hell-cats.'

I finished fixing the cut. James Bond had been watching cabin Number 1. Now he said, 'Better get under cover. They may have got something heavy in there, and they'll have finished fixing the Horror's foot.' He got to his feet. He suddenly yanked my arm, and said, 'Quick!' At the same time I heard the tinkle of glass away on the right and a deafening rattle that I supposed was some kind of machine-gun. On our heels, bullets whipped into the side of the lobby building.

James Bond smiled. 'Sorry again, Viv! My reactions don't seem all that smart tonight. I'll do better.' He paused. 'Now, let's just think for a minute.'

It was a long minute, and I was sweating with the heat from the burning lobby. Now there was only the north wall and the bit we were sheltering behind as far as the front door. The rest was a mass of flames. But the wind was still blowing the fire southwards and it seemed to me that this last bit of masonry might stand up a long while yet. Most of the cabins were on their way to burning out and, on that side of the clearing, there was a lessening of the glare and sparks. It crossed my mind that the blaze must have been visible for miles, perhaps even as far as Lake George or Glens Falls, yet no one had turned up to help. Probably the highway patrols and the fire services had enough on their hands with the havoc caused by the storm. And, as for their beloved forests, they would reckon that no fire could spread through this soaking landscape.

James Bond said, 'Now this is what we're going to do. First of all, I want you somewhere where you can help but where I don't have to worry about you. Otherwise, if I know these men, they'll concentrate on you and guess that I'll do anything, even let them get away, rather than let you get hurt.'

'Is that true?'

'Don't be silly. So you get on over the road under cover of this bit of building and then work back, keeping well out of sight, until you're just about opposite their car. Stay quiet, and even if one or both of them gets to the car, hold your fire until I tell you to shoot. All right?'

'But where will you be?'

'We've got what are known as interior lines of defence—if we consider the cars as the objective. I'm going to stick around here and let them come at me. It's they who want to get us and get away. Let 'em try. Time's against them.' He looked at his watch. 'It's nearly three. How long before first light around here?'

'About two hours. Around five. But there are two of them and only one of you! They'll do a sort of what they call "pincers movement".'

'One of the crabs has lost a claw. Anyway, that's the best I can do for a master plan. Now you get on across the road before they start something. I'll keep them occupied.'

He went to the corner of the building, edged round and took two quick shots at the right-hand cabin. There was a distant crash of glass and then the vicious blast of the sub-machine-gun. Bullets splatted into the masonry and whipped across the road into the trees. James Bond had pulled back. He smiled encouragingly. 'Now!'

I ran to the right and across the road, keeping the lobby building between me and the end cabin, and scrambled in among the trees. Once again they tore and scratched at me, but now I had proper shoes on and the material of the overalls was tough. I got well inside the wood and then began working along to the left. When I thought I had gone far enough I crept down towards the light from the flames. I ended up where I had wanted to, just inside the first line of trees with the black sedan about twenty yards away on the other side of the road and a fairly clear view of the flickering battlefield.

All this while, the moon had been dodging in and out through the scudding clouds—in turns lighting everything brightly and then switching itself off and leaving only the changing glare that came mostly from the blazing left half of the lobby block. Now the moon came fully out and showed me something that almost made me scream. The thin man, crawling on his stomach, was worming his way up the north side of the lobby block and the moonlight glinted on the gun in his hand.

James Bond was where I had left him and, to keep him there, Sluggsy now kept up a steady stream of single shots that flicked every few seconds at the angle of the wall towards which the thin man was worming his way. Perhaps James Bond guessed the significance of this steady fire. He may have known that it was meant to pin him down, because now he began moving along to the left, towards the burning half of the building. And now he was running, bent low, out across the browned grass and through the billowing smoke and sparks towards the charred, flickering ruins of the left-hand line of cabins. I caught a brief glimpse of him diving through one of the car-ports at around Number 15 and then he was gone, presumably into the trees at the back to work his way up and take Sluggsy in the rear.

I watched the thin man. He was nearly at the corner of the building. Now he was there. The single shots ceased. Without taking aim, and firing with his left hand, the thin man edged his gun round the corner and sprayed a whole magazine, blind, down the front wall where James and I had been standing.

When no answering fire came, he jerked his head round the corner and back again, like a snake, and then got to his feet and made a sweeping motion with his hand to show that we had gone.

And now there came two quick shots from the direction of cabin Number 1 followed by a blood-curdling scream that stopped my heart, and Sluggsy came backing out on to the lawn, firing from the hip with his right while his left hand dangled down at his side. He continued to run backwards, screaming with pain, but still firing his machine-gun in short bursts, and then I saw a flicker of movement in one of the car-ports and there came the deep answering boom of the heavy automatic. But Sluggsy switched his aim and James Bond's guns went silent. Then they began again from another place and one of the shots must have hit the machine-gun because Sluggsy suddenly dropped it and began to run towards the black sedan where the thin man was crouching, giving long-range covering fire with two guns. James Bond's hit on the sub-machine-gun must have jammed the mechanism for it went on firing, jerking round like a flaming catherine wheel in the grass and spraying bullets all over the place. And then the thin man was in the driving seat and I heard the engine catch and a spurt of smoke came from the exhaust, and he flung open the side door and Sluggsy got to it and the door was slammed on him by the forward leap of the car.

I didn't wait for James. I ran out into the road and began blazing away at the back of the car and heard some of my bullets wham into the metal. Then the hammer clicked on nothing, and I stood and swore at the thought of them getting away. But then came the steady crash of James's gun from the far side of the lawn while fire spat back from the front window of the car. Until all of a sudden the black sedan seemed to go crazy. It made a wide swerve and looked to be heading across the lawn straight for James. For a moment he was caught in its great lights as he stood there, the sweat gleaming on his naked chest, and fired, in the classic stance of the dueller, as if at a charging animal. I thought he was going to be mown down and I began to run across the grass towards him, but then the car veered away and, its engine roaring in bottom gear, made straight for the lake.

I stood and watched, fascinated. Thereabouts the lawn was

cut to the edge of a low cliff, about twenty feet high, below which is a fishing pool, and there were some rough-hewn benches and tables for people to sit and picnic. The car tore on, and now, whether or not it hit a bench, its speed would certainly get it to the lake. But it missed all the benches and, as I put my hand up to my mouth in horrified excitement, it took off over the edge and landed flat on the water with a giant splash and crash of metal and glass. Then, quite slowly, it sank, nose down, in a welter of exhaust gas and bubbles, until there was nothing left but the trunk and a section of the roof and rear window slanting up towards the sky.

James Bond was still standing, gazing at the lake, when I ran up to him and threw my arms round him. 'Are you all right? Are you hurt?'

He turned dazedly towards me and put his arm round my waist and held me tight. He said vaguely, 'No. I'm all right.' He looked back towards the lake. 'I must have hit the driver, the thin man. Killed him, and his body jammed the accelerator.' He seemed to come to himself. He smiled tautly. 'Well, that's certainly tidied up the situation. No ragged edges to clean up. Dead and buried all in one go. Can't say I'm sorry. They were a couple of real thugs.' He let go of me and thrust his gun up into its holster. He smelled of cordite and sweat. It was delicious. I reached up and kissed him.

We turned away and walked slowly across the grass. The fire was only burning fitfully now and the battlefield was almost dark. My watch said it was three thirty. I suddenly felt utterly, absolutely finished.

As if echoing my thoughts, James said. 'That's worked the Benzedrine off. How about getting a little sleep? There are still four or five cabins in good shape. How about 2 and 3? Are they desirable suites?'

I felt myself blushing. I said obstinately, 'I don't mind what you think, James, but I'm not going to leave you tonight. You can choose either 2 or 3. I'll sleep on the floor.'

He laughed, and reached out and hugged me to him. 'If you sleep on the floor, I'll sleep on the floor too. But it seems rather a waste of a fine double bed. Let's say Number 3.' He stopped and looked at me, pretending to be polite. 'Or would you rather have Number 2?'

'No. Number 3 would be heavenly.'

Cabin Number 3 was airless and stuffy. While James Bond collected our 'luggage' from among the trees, I opened the glass slats of the windows and turned down the sheets on the double bed. I should have felt embarrassed, but I didn't. I just enjoyed housekeeping for him by moonlight. Then I tried the shower and found miraculously that there was still full pressure, though further down the line many stretches of the pipes must have melted. The top cabins were nearer to the main. I stripped off all my clothes and made them into a neat pile and went into the shower and opened a new cake of Camay ('Pamper your Guests with Pink Camay—With a scent like costly French Perfume . . . blended with Fine Cold Cream' I remembered, because it sounded so succulent, it said on the packet) and began to lather myself all over, gently, because of the bruises.

Through the noise of the shower, I didn't hear him come into the bathroom. But suddenly there were two more hands washing me and a naked body was up against mine and I smelled the sweat and the gunpowder and I turned and laughed up into his grimy face and then I was in his arms and our mouths met in a kiss that seemed as if it would never end while the water poured down and made us shut our eyes.

When my breath was almost exhausted, he pulled me out

from under the shower and we kissed again, more slowly, while his hands wandered over my body and desire came in waves of dizziness. I simply couldn't stand it. I said, 'Please, James! Please don't! Or I shall fall down. And be gentle. You're hurting me.'

In the moonlit dusk of the bathroom, his eyes were only fierce slits. Now they relaxed into tenderness and laughter. 'I'm sorry, Viv. It's not my fault. It's my hands. They won't stay away from you. And they ought to be washing *me*. I'm filthy. You'll have to do it. They won't obey me.'

I laughed up at him, and pulled him under the shower. 'All right then. But I shan't be gentle. The last time I washed anyone it was a pony when I was about twelve! Anyway, I can hardly see which bit of you's which!' I got hold of the soap. 'Put your face down. I'll try not to put too much in your eyes.'

'If you put any in, I'll . . .' My hands stopped the rest of the sentence and I set about scrubbing his face and hair and then moved on down his arms and chest, while he stood bowed and holding with both hands to the water pipe.

I stopped. 'You'll have to do the rest.'

'Certainly not. And do it properly. You never know. There might be a world war and you'd have to be a nurse. You might as well learn how to wash a man. And anyway, what the hell's this soap? I smell like Cleopatra.'

'It's very good. It's got costly French perfume in it. It says so on the packet. And you smell delicious. Much better than your gunpowder smell.'

He laughed. 'Well, get on. But hurry.'

So I bent down and began and of course in a minute we were in each other's arms again under the shower and our bodies were slithery with water and soap and he turned the shower off and lifted me out of the shower cabinet and began to dry me lingeringly with the bath towel while I leant back within his free arm and just let it happen. Then I took the towel and dried him, and then it was silly to wait any longer and he picked me up in his arms and carried me through into the bedroom and laid me down on the bed and I watched through half-closed lashes his pale shape as he went round drawing the curtains and locking up.

And then he was lying beside me.

His hands and his mouth were slow and electric and his body in my arms was tenderly fierce.

Afterwards he told me that when the moment came I screamed. I didn't know I had. I only know that a chasm of piercing sweetness suddenly opened and drowned me and that I dug my nails into his hips to make sure of taking him with me. Then he sleepily said some sweet things and kissed me once and his body slithered away and lay still and I stayed on my back and gazed up into the red darkness and listened to his breathing.

I had never before made love, full love, with my heart as well as my body. It had been sweet with Derek, cold and satisfying with Kurt. But this was something different. At last I realized what this thing could be in one's life.

I think I know why I gave myself so completely to this man, how I was capable of it with someone I had met only six hours before. Apart from the excitement of his looks, his authority, his maleness, he had come from nowhere, like the prince in the fairy tales, and he had saved me from the dragon. But for him, I would now be dead, after suffering God knows what before. He could have changed the wheel on his car and gone off, or, when danger came, he could have saved his own skin. But he had fought for my life as if it had been his own. And then, when the dragon was dead, he had taken me as his reward. In a few hours, I knew, he would be gone—without protestations of love, without apologies or excuses. And that would be the end of that—gone, finished.

All women love semi-rape. They love to be taken. It was his sweet brutality against my bruised body that had made his act of love so piercingly wonderful. That and the coinciding of nerves completely relaxed after the removal of tension and danger, the warmth of gratitude, and a woman's natural feeling for her hero. I had no regrets and no shame. There might be many consequences for me—not the least that I might now be dissatisfied with other men. But whatever my troubles were, he would never hear of them. I would not pursue him and try to repeat what there had been between us. I would stay away from him and leave him to go his own road where there would be other women, countless other women, who would probably give him as much physical pleasure as he had had with me. I wouldn't care, or at least I told myself that I wouldn't care, because none of them would ever own him—own any larger piece of him than I now did. And for all my life I would be grateful to him, for everything. And I would remember him for ever as my image of a man.

How silly could one be? What was there to dramatize about this naked male person lying beside me? He was just a professional agent who had done his job. He was trained to fire guns, to kill people. What was so wonderful about that? Brave, strong, ruthless with women—these were the qualities that went with his calling—what he was paid to be. He was only some kind of a spy, a spy who had loved me. Not even loved, slept with. Why should I make him my hero, swear never to forget him? I suddenly had an impulse to wake him up and ask him: 'Can you be nice? Can you be kind?'

I turned over on my side. He was asleep, breathing quietly, his head resting on his outflung forearm, his right arm tucked under the pillow. Again the moon outside was bright. Red light filtered through the curtains, mixing the black shadows of his body with shining crimson highlights. I bent closely over him, breathing in his maleness, longing to touch him, to run my hand down his sunburned back to where the brown became abruptly white where his summer bathing-trunks had been.

After looking long at him, I lay back. No, he was as I had thought him to be. Yes, this was a man to love.

The red curtains at the other end of the room were moving. Through half-sleeping eyes I wondered why. Outside, the wind had dropped and there was no sound. Lazily I raised my eyes to look above me. The curtains at this end of the room, above our bed, were motionless. There must be a small breeze coming off the lake. Come on! For heaven's sake go to sleep!

And then, with a sudden ripping noise high up on the opposite wall, the bits of curtain hung sideways. And a big, glittering turnip-face, pale and shiny under the moon, was looking through the glass slats!

I never knew that hair could stand up on end. I thought it was invented by writers. But I heard a scratching on the pillow round my ears and I felt the fresh night air on my scalp. 'I wanted to scream, but I couldn't.' 'My limbs were frozen.' 'I couldn't move hand or foot.' I thought these too were fictions. They aren't. I simply lay and stared, noting my physical sensations—even to the symptom that my eyes were so wide open that they ached. But I couldn't move a finger. I was—another phrase from books—frightened stiff, stiff as a board.

The face behind the glass window slats was grinning. Perhaps the teeth were bared, like an animal's, with effort. The moon glistened off the teeth and off the eyes and off the top of the hairless head to make a kind of child's sketch of a face.

The ghost face jerked slowly round the room, looking. It

saw the white bed with the twin smudges of the heads on the pillow. It stopped looking and slowly, painfully, a hand, with shiny metal in it, came up beside the head and smashed clumsily downwards through the panes of glass.

The noise was a trigger that released me. I screamed and hit sideways with my hand. It probably didn't help. The crash of glass had wakened him. I might even have spoiled his aim. But then came the double roar of guns, the solid slap of bullets into the wall above my head, another great splintering of glass and the turnip face had gone.

'Are you all right, Viv?' His voice was urgent, desperate.

He saw that I was and didn't wait for an answer. The bed heaved and suddenly the moonlight threw a great block of light through the door. He ran so quietly that I didn't hear his feet on the concrete floor of the car-port, but I could visualize him flattening himself against its wall and edging round. I just lay and stared aghast—another literary word, but an accurate one—at the jagged remains of the window and remembered the glistening, horrible turnip head that must have been a ghost.

James Bond came back. He didn't say a word. The first thing he did was to get me a glass of water. The prosaic action, the first thing a parent does when the child has nightmares, brought back the room and its familiar shapes from the black and red cave of the ghosts and the guns. Then he fetched a bath towel and put a chair under the smashed window and climbed on it and draped the towel over the window.

I was suddenly conscious of the muscles that bunched and relaxed in his naked body and I was amused at how odd a man looks without any clothes on when he is not making love but just moving about a room doing kind of household chores. I thought that perhaps one ought to be a nudist. But perhaps only under forty. I said, 'James, don't ever get fat.'

He had fixed the towel as a curtain. He got down off the chair and said absent-mindedly, 'No. That's right. One shouldn't get fat.'

He put the chair tidily back beside the desk where it belonged and picked up his gun that he had put down on the desk. He examined the gun. He went to his small pile of clothes and took out a new clip and substituted it for the old one and came over to the bed and slipped the gun under his pillow.

Now I realized why he had lain like that, with his right hand doubled under the pillow. I guessed that he always slept like that. I thought his must be rather like a fireman's life, always waiting for a call. I thought how extraordinary it must be to have danger as your business.

He came and sat down on the edge of my side of the bed. In the filtering scraps of light his face looked drawn and sort of blasted, as if by shock. He tried to smile, but the tense muscles wouldn't let him and it was only a crooked sketch of a smile. He said, 'I nearly got us both killed again. I'm sorry, Viv. I must be losing my touch. If I go on like this I'm going to catch trouble. When the car went into the lake, remember a bit of the roof and the rear window was left sticking out of the water? Well, there was obviously plenty of air trapped in that corner. I was a damned fool not to have worked that out for myself. This fellow Sluggsy only needed to knock out the rear window and swim ashore. He was hit several times. It must have been hard going for him. But he got to our cabin. We ought to be dead ducks. Don't go round the back in the morning. He's not a pretty sight.' He looked at me for reassurance. 'Anyway, I'm sorry, Viv. It ought never to have happened.'

I scrambled off the bed and went and put my arms round him. His body was cold. I hugged him to me and kissed him. 'Don't be silly, James! If it wasn't for me, you wouldn't have got into all this mess. And where would I be now if it wasn't for you? I'd not only have been a dead duck, but a roasted one too, hours ago. The trouble with you is you haven't had enough sleep. And you're cold. Come into bed with me. I'll keep you warm.' I got up and pulled him to his feet.

He caught me to him. He reached down with both hands and pressed my body hard into his. He held me like that for a time, quite still, and I felt the way his body was gaining warmth from mine. Then he lifted me up and laid me softly back on the bed. And then he took me fiercely, almost cruelly, and once again there came the small scream from someone who was no longer me and then we were lying side by side and his heart was pounding wildly against my breast and I found that my right hand was clenched in his hair.

I relaxed my cramped fingers and reached down for his hand. I said, 'James, what's a bimbo?'

'Why?'

'I'll tell you when you've told me.'

He laughed sleepily. 'It's gangster language for a whore.'

'I thought it was something like that. They kept on calling me that. I suppose it must really be true.'

'You don't qualify.'

'Promise you don't think I'm a bimbo?'

'Promise. You're just a darling chick. I'm cow-simple about you.'

'What's that mean?'

'It means crazy for a girl. Now, that's enough questions. Go to sleep.' He kissed me gently, and turned over on his side.

I curled up against him, fitting myself close in to his back and thighs. 'This is a nice way to sleep—like spoons. Goodnight, James.'

'Goodnight, darling Viv.'

15 / *THE WRITING ON MY HEART*

Those were the last words he spoke to me. When I woke up the next morning he was gone. There was only the dent down the bed where he had lain, and the smell of him on the pillow. To make sure, I jumped out of bed and ran to see if the grey car was still there. It wasn't.

It was a beautiful day and there was heavy dew on the ground, and in the dew I could see the single track of his footprints leading to where the car had been. A bobolink flew crying across the clearing, and from somewhere in the trees came the dying call of a mourning dove.

The ruins of the motel were black and hideous and a ghostly wisp of smoke rose straight up into the still air from the remains of the lobby block. I went back into the cabin and had a shower and began briskly to pack my things into my saddle-bags. Then I saw the letter on the dressing table and I went and sat on the bed and read it.

It was written on motel paper from the writing desk. The writing was very clear and even and he had used a real pen and not a ball point.

Dear Viv,

You may have to show this to the police, so I will be businesslike. I am on my way to Glens Falls where I will make a full report to the police after telling the Highway Patrol to get to you immediately. I will also get in touch with Washington and they will almost certainly put Albany in charge of the case. I shall pull every string to see that you are not worried too much and that they let you go on your way after getting your statement. Glens Falls will have my route and the registration number of the car and they will be able to pick me up wherever I am if you need any help or they want to know anything more from me. You won't be able to get any breakfast so I shall have the Patrol bring you a Thermos of coffee and sandwiches to keep you alive. I would much like to stay with you, if only to see Mr Sanguinetti! But I very much doubt if he will be turning up this morning. I guess that when he heard nothing from his two strong-arm boys he went like hell to Albany and got on the first plane for the south on his way out to Mexico. I shall tell Washington that that's my guess and they should be able to pick him up if they get a move on. He should get life for this, or what's known as 'from now on', or 'The Rosary', in the language we've been learning. And now listen. You, and up to a point me, have saved the insurance company at least half a million dollars and there'll be a big reward. I'm not allowed to accept rewards by the rules of my job, so there's no argument about that, even if it weren't a fact that it was you who took the principal burden of all this and it's you who are the heroine. So I'm going to make a real issue of this and see that the insurance company does the right thing. And something else. I wouldn't be at all surprised if one or both of those hoodlums wasn't wanted by the police and has a reward on his head. I'll see to that too. As for the future, drive very carefully the rest of the way. And don't have nightmares. These sort of things don't often happen. Treat it all as just a bad motor accident you were lucky to get out of. And go on being as wonderful as you are. If you ever want me or need any help, wherever you are, you can get me by letter or cable, but not by telephone, c/o Ministry of Defence, Storey's Gate, London, SW1.

Ever,

J.B.

PS. Your tyre pressures are too high for the South. Remember to take them down.

PPS. Try Guerlain's 'Fleurs des Alpes' instead of Camay!

I heard the roar of motor-cycles coming up the road. When they stopped, there was the brief wail of a siren to announce who they were. I put the letter inside the top of my overalls and pulled up the zip and went out to meet The Law.

They were two State Troopers, smart and young and very nice. I'd almost forgotten such people existed. They saluted me as if I was royalty. 'Miss Vivienne Michel?' The senior, a lieutenant, did the talking while his Number Two muttered quietly into his radio announcing their arrival.

'Yes.'

'I'm Lieutenant Morrow. We hear you had some trouble last night.' He gestured with his gloved hand at the ruins. 'Seems like we heard right.'

'Oh, that's nothing,' I said disdainfully. 'There's a car in the lake with a corpse in it and another corpse behind cabin Number 3.'

'Yes, miss.' There was a hint of disapproval at my levity. He turned to his companion, who had clipped back the microphone to the set behind his saddle. 'O'Donnell, take a look round, would you?'

'Okay, loot.' O'Donnell strode off across the grass.

'Well, let's go and take a seat somewhere, Miss Michel.' The lieutenant bent down to one of his saddle-bags and produced a carefully wrapped package. 'Brought along some breakfast. 'Fraid it's only coffee and doughnuts. That suit you?' He held out the package.

I gave him a full candlepower smile. 'That's terribly kind of you. I'm starving. There are some seats over by the lake. We can choose one that's out of sight of the sunk car.' I led the way across the grass and we sat down. The lieutenant took off his cap and produced a notebook and pencil and pretended to go through his notes to give me a chance to get started on a doughnut.

He looked up and produced his first smile. 'Now don't worry about this, miss. I'm not taking a statement. The captain's coming up himself for that. Should be along any time now. When they gave me the hurry call I got down the bare facts. But what's worrying me is that that radio just hasn't left me alone since then. Had to cut down my speed the whole way here from Route 9 to keep on listening to instructions from the station—that Albany was interested in the case, that even the top brass in Washington was breathing down our necks. Never heard such a load coming over the air. Now, miss, can you tell me how it's come about that Washington's mixed up in this, and within a bare couple of hours of Glens Falls getting the first report?'

I couldn't help smiling at his earnestness. I could almost hear him calling over to O'Donnell as they roared along, 'Hell, we'll have Jack Kennedy on our tails any moment now!' I said, 'Well, there's a man called James Bond who's involved. He saved me and shot these two gangsters. He's some kind of an English agent, secret service or something. He was driving from Toronto to Washington to report on a case, and he got a flat and ended up at the motel. If he hadn't, I'd be dead by now. Anyway, I guess he must be someone pretty important. He told me he wanted to make sure this Mr Sanguinetti didn't get away to Mexico or somewhere. But that's more or less all I know about him, except that—except that he seemed a wonderful guy.'

The lieutenant looked sympathetic. 'Guess so, miss. If he got you out of this trouble. But he's certainly got a fix in with the FBI. They don't often tangle in a local case like this. Unless they're called in, that is, or there's some Federal angle.' The thin wail of sirens sounded far down the road. Lieutenant Morrow got to his feet and put his cap on. 'Well thanks, miss. I was just satisfying my curiosity. The captain will be taking over from here. Don't you worry. He's a nice kind of a guy.' O'Donnell came up. 'If you'll excuse me, miss.' The lieutenant moved off with O'Donnell, listening to his report, and I finished the coffee and followed slowly, thinking of the grey Thunderbird that would now be hammering out the miles southward and of the sunburned hands on the wheel.

It was quite a cavalcade that came sweeping up the road between the pines—a squad car with outriders, an ambulance, two other police cars and a recovery truck that came towards me across the grass and went on down to the lake. Everyone seemed to have had their orders, and very soon the whole area was covered with moving figures in olive green or dark blue.

The heavily-built man who soon came forward to meet me, followed by a junior officer who turned out to be the stenographer, looked every inch the detective-captain of the films—slow-moving, kindly-faced, purposeful. He held out his hand. 'Miss Michel? I'm Captain Stonor from Glens Falls. Let's go somewhere where we can have a talk, shall we? One of the cabins, or shall we stay out in the open?'

'I've had about enough of the cabins, if you don't mind. Why not over there—my breakfast table. And by the way, thank you very much for your thoughtfulness. I was starving.'

'Don't thank me, Miss Michel,' the captain's eyes twinkled frostily. 'It was your English friend, Commander Bond, who suggested it,' he paused, 'among other things.'

So he was a commander. It was the only rank I liked the name of. And of course he was bound to have put the captain's back up—an Englishman with all this authority. And with the CIA and FBI of all people! Nothing would irritate the regular police more. I decided to be extremely diplomatic.

We sat down and, after the usual police preliminaries, I was asked to tell my story.

It took two hours, what with Captain Stonor's questions and men coming up from time to time to whisper hoarsely into his ear, and at the end of it I was exhausted. Coffee was brought and cigarettes for me ('Not while I'm on duty, thank you, Miss Michel'), and then we all relaxed and the stenographer was sent away. Captain Stonor sent for Lieutenant Morrow and took him aside to radio a preliminary report to headquarters, and I watched the wreck of the black sedan, that had by now been hauled up the cliff, being towed over the lawn to the road. There the ambulance was driven over beside it, and I turned away as a wet bundle was carefully lifted out on to the grass. Horror! I remembered again those cold, red-flecked eyes. I felt his hands on me. Could it have happened?

I heard the captain say, 'And copies to Albany and Washington. Right?' And then he was back sitting opposite me.

He looked at me kindly and said some complimentary things. I looked appreciative and said, 'No, no.' I asked when he thought I could get on.

Captain Stonor didn't answer immediately. Instead he slowly reached up and took off his cap and put it on the table. The armistice gesture, a copy of the lieutenant's, made me smile inside. Then he rummaged in his pockets and took out cigarettes and a lighter. He offered me one and then lit his own. He smiled at me, his first non-official smile. 'I'm going off duty now, Miss Michel.' He sat back comfortably and crossed his legs, resting his left ankle on his right knee and holding the ankle. He suddenly looked like a middle-aged man with a family, taking it easy. He took his first long draw on his cigarette and watched the smoke drift away. He said, 'You can be going any time now, Miss Michel. Your friend Commander Bond was anxious that you should be put to as little trouble as possible. And I'm glad to accommodate him—and you. And,' he smiled with unexpected humour and irony,

'I didn't need Washington to add their wishes in this matter. You've been a brave girl. You got involved in a bad crime and you behaved like I'd wish any child of mine to behave. Those two hoodlums are both wanted men. I'll be putting in your name for the rewards. Likewise to the insurance company, who will certainly be generous. We've booked those Phanceys on a preliminary charge of conspiracy to defraud, and this Mr Sanguinetti is already on the run, as the Commander suggested this morning he would be. We checked with Troy, as we would have checked anyway, and the normal police machinery is in motion to pick him up. There will be a capital charge against Mr Sanguinetti, if and when we catch up with him, and it may be that you will be needed as a material witness. The State will pay for you to be brought from wherever you may be, housed and taken back again. All this,' Captain Stonor made a throwaway gesture with his cigarette, 'is normal police routine and it will look after itself.' The astute blue eyes looked carefully into mine and then veiled themselves. 'But that doesn't quite end the case to my satisfaction.' He smiled. 'That is, now that I'm off duty, so to speak, and there's only just you and me.'

I tried to look just interested and nonchalant, but I wondered what was coming.

'Did this Commander Bond leave you any instructions, any letter? He told me that he had left you asleep early this morning. That he had gone off around six and had not wanted to wake you up. Quite right of course. But,' Captain Stonor examined the end of his cigarette, 'your evidence and the Commander's is to the effect that you shared the same cabin. Quite natural in the circumstances. You wouldn't have wanted to be alone any more last night. But it seems rather an abrupt goodbye—after an exciting night like that. No trouble with him, I suppose? He didn't, er, try to get fresh with you, if you get my meaning?' The eyes were apologetic, but they probed into mine.

I blushed furiously. I said sharply, 'Certainly not, Captain. Yes, he did leave a letter for me. A perfectly straightforward one. I didn't mention it because it doesn't add anything to what you know.' I ran down the zip on my front and reached inside for the letter, blushing even worse. Damn the man!

He took the letter and read it carefully. He handed it back. 'A very nice letter. Very, er, businesslike. I don't get the bit about the soap.'

I said shortly, 'Oh, that was only a joke about the motel soap. He said it was too strongly scented.'

'I see. Yes, sure. Well, that's fine, Miss Michel.' The eyes were kindly again. 'Well, now. D'you mind if I say something personal? Talk to you a minute as if you might be my own daughter? You could be, you know—almost my granddaughter if I'd started early enough.' He chuckled cosily.

'No. Please say anything you like.'

Captain Stonor took another cigarette and lit it. 'Well, now, Miss Michel, what the Commander says is right. You've been in the equivalent of a bad motor accident and you don't want to have any nightmares about it. But there's more to it than that. You've been suddenly introduced, out of the blue so to speak, and violently, to the underground war of crime, the war that's going on all the time and that you read about and see in movies. And, like in the movies, the cop has rescued the maiden from the robbers.' He leant forward across the table and held my eyes firmly in his. 'Now don't get me wrong about this, Miss Michel, and if I'm speaking out of turn just forget what I'm going to say. But it would be unreasonable of you not to create a hero out of the cop who saved you, perhaps build an image in your mind that that's the sort of man to look up to, even perhaps to want to marry.' The captain sat back.

He smiled apologetically. 'Now the reason I'm going into all this is because violent emergencies like what you've been through leave their scars. They're one hell of a shock to anyone—to any dam' citizen. But most of all to a young person like yourself. Now I believe,' (the kind eyes became less kind) 'I have good reason from the reports of my officers to believe, that you had intimate relations with Commander Bond last night. I'm afraid it's one of our less attractive duties to be able to read such signs.' Captain Stonor held up his hand. 'Now I'm not prying any more into these private things, and they're none of my business, but it would be perfectly natural, almost inevitable, that you might have lost your heart, or at any rate part of it, to this personable young Englishman who has just saved your life.' The sympathy in the fatherly smile was edged with irony. 'After all's said and done, that's what happens in the books and in the movies, isn't it? So why not in real life?'

I stirred impatiently, wanting this stupid lecture to finish, wanting to be gone.

'Now I'm coming to the end very quickly, Miss Michel, and I know you think I'm being very impertinent, but ever since I got past middle-age on the force, I've been interested in what I call post-natal care after a case like this. Particularly when the survivor is young and might be damaged by what the young person has been through. So I want to leave one thought with you if I may, and then wish you the best of luck and a happy journey on that crazy little scooter-thing of yours. It's just this, Miss Michel.'

Captain Stonor's eyes continued to look into mine, but they had lost focus. I knew I was going to hear something from the heart. This is a rare thing between generations—between grown-ups and children. I stopped thinking of getting away and paid attention.

'This underground war I was talking about, this crime battle that's always going on—whether it's being fought between cops and robbers or between spies and counter-spies. This is a private battle between two trained armies, one fighting on the side of law and of what his own country thinks is right, and one belonging to the enemies of these things.' Captain Stonor was now talking to himself. I imagined that he was reciting something—something he felt very strongly about—perhaps had said in speeches or in an article in some police magazine. 'But in the higher ranks of these forces, among the toughest of the professionals, there's a deadly quality in the persons involved which is common to both—to both friends and enemies.' The captain's closed first came softly down on the wooden table-top for emphasis, and his inward-looking eyes burned with a dedicated, private anger. 'The top gangsters, the top FBI operatives, the top spies and the top counter-spies are cold-hearted, cold-blooded, ruthless, tough, killers, Miss Michel. Yes, even the "friends" as opposed to the "enemies". They have to be. They wouldn't survive if they weren't. Do you get me?' Captain Stonor's eyes came back into focus. Now they held mine with a friendly urgency that touched my feelings—but not, I'm ashamed to say, my heart. 'So the message I want to leave with you, my dear—and I've talked with Washington and I've learned something about Commander Bond's outstanding record in his particular line of business—is this. Keep away from *all* these men. They are not for you, whether they're called James Bond or Sluggsy Morant. Both these men, and others like them, belong to a private jungle into which you've strayed for a few hours and from which you've escaped. So don't go and get sweet dreams about the one or nightmares from the other. They're just different people from the likes of you—a different species.' Captain Stonor smiled, 'Like hawks and doves, if you'll pardon the comparison. Get me?' My expression cannot have been receptive. The voice became abrupt. 'Okay, let's go then.'

Captain Stonor got to his feet and I followed. I didn't know what to say. I remembered my immediate reaction when James Bond had shown himself at the door of the motel—'Oh, God, it's another of them.' But I also remembered his smile and his kisses and his arm round me. I walked meekly beside this large, comfortable man who had come out with these kindly-meant thoughts, and all I could think was that I wanted a big lunch and then a long sleep at least a hundred miles from The Dreamy Pines Motor Court.

It was twelve noon by the time I got away. Captain Stonor said I was going to have a lot of trouble from the press, but that he would stave them off for as long as possible. I could say all I wished about James Bond except what his profession was and where he could be found. He was just a man who had turned up at the right time and then gone on his way.

I had packed my saddle-bags and the young State Trooper, Lieutenant Morrow, strapped them on for me and wheeled the Vespa out on to the road. On the way over the lawn he said, 'Mind out for the potholes between here and Glens Falls, miss. Some of them are so deep you better sound your horn before you get to them. There might be other folks with little machines like this at the bottom of them.' I laughed. He was clean and gay and young, but tough and adventurous as well by the looks of him and from his job. Perhaps this was more the type of man I should build dreams about!

I said goodbye to Captain Stonor and thanked him. Then, rather frightened of making a fool of myself, I put on my crash helmet and pulled down my saucy, fur-lined goggles, got on the machine and stamped on the starter pedal. Thank heavens the little engine fired right away! Now I would show them! By design, the rear wheel was still on its stand. I let in the clutch fairly fast and gave a quick push. The spinning rear wheel made contact with the loose surface of the road, and dust and pebbles flew. And I was gone like a rocket and, in ten seconds through the gears, I was doing forty. The surface looked all right ahead so I took a chance and glanced back and raised a cheeky hand in farewell, and there was a wave from the little group of police in front of the smoking lobby block. And then I was off down the long straight road between the two sentinel rows of pine trees and I thought the trees looked sorry to be letting me get away unharmed.

Unharmed? What was it the captain of detectives had said about 'scars'? I just didn't believe him. The scars of my terror had been healed, wiped away, by this stranger who slept with a gun under his pillow, this secret agent who was only known by a number.

A secret agent? I didn't care what he did. A number? I had already forgotten it. I knew exactly who he was and what he was. And everything, every smallest detail, would be written on my heart for ever.

read more 

PENGUIN MODERN CLASSICS

CASINO ROYALE, LIVE AND LET DIE, MOONRAKER
IAN FLEMING

'The most forceful and driving writer of thrillers in England' Raymond Chandler

With *Casino Royale*, Ian Fleming introduced Commander James Bond, the archetypal secret agent: debonair, ruthless and licensed to kill. This volume contains the first three superb Bond adventures, which find 007 up against deadly Russian spy Le Chiffre, whom Bond must force into retirement by ruining at baccarat; trailing SMERSH operative Mr Big to the Caribbean, where beautiful, fortune-telling Solitaire is kept prisoner; and uncovering just what lies behind the Moonraker project led by powerful millionaire Sir Hugo Drax …

'Nobody does this sort of thing as well as Mr Fleming' *Sunday Times*

With an Introduction by Candia McWilliam

---

read more 

PENGUIN MODERN CLASSICS

FROM RUSSIA WITH LOVE, DR NO, GOLDFINGER
IAN FLEMING

'Fleming is splendid; he stops at nothing' *New Statesman*

With the creation of suave secret agent James Bond, Ian Fleming invented one of the most iconic heroes ever to appear in print or on film. This volume contains three of the greatest Bond novels, full of the dazzling plots and arch-villains that made 007 a phenomenon. Here Bond encounters ravishing agent Tatiana Romanova and fiendish Rosa Klebb in Russia; becomes trapped in Dr No's tropical lair with beautiful Honey Rider; and confronts ruthless criminal Auric Goldfinger, whose lethal schemes involve fifteen billion dollars' worth of gold …

'Possibly the best Ian Fleming thriller … Rosa Klebb is a female unparalleled for awfulness. From beginning to end here's magnificent writing' Elizabeth Bowen on *From Russia with Love*

With an Introduction by Christopher Hitchens

PENGUIN MODERN CLASSICS

ON HER MAJESTY'S SECRET SERVICE
IAN FLEMING

'Fleming is in a class by himself' *Daily Mail*

'If there was one thing that set James Bond really moving, it was being passed at speed by a pretty girl ...'

From the moment he first meets Teresa di Vicenzo – a reckless playgirl with a love of fast cars and danger – Bond is fascinated. She also leads him to new information on one of the most dangerous criminals in the world, Ernst Stavro Blofeld. In his Alpine mountain base, Blofeld is developing weapons that could threaten the whole world. Only 007 – with the help of someone who can handle herself at speed – can stop the evil genius. Filled with ski chases, schnapps and snow-bound lairs, *On Her Majesty's Secret Service* also shows confirmed bachelor Bond's icy reserve finally melting ...
